SUDDENLY LILY

SUDDENLY LILY

•

Deborah Nolan

Montlake
Romance

Text copyright ©2009 by Deborah M. Nolan
Printed in the United States of America.

Published by Montlake Romance
P.O. Box 400818
Las Vegas, NV 89140

ISBN-13: 9781477813966
ISBN-10: 1477813969

This book is dedicated to my husband Frank.
Without his encouragement I would not
have kept writing, and to my children:
Frank, Nora and Sarah, whose own searches and
dreams remind me to keep pursuing mine.

This book is also dedicated to the real heroes
of this book: the women and men in the state
of New Jersey who work in child welfare,
including DYFS workers, Deputy Attorney
Generals, Law Guardians, Public Defenders
and Family Court Judges, all who have dedicated
their lives to keeping our children safe.

Without the steadfast support and grammatical skills of my writing partners, Joani Ascher and Kim Zito, my writing career would remain an idea rather than a reality.

Chapter One

Sheriff Michael Frascato had just picked up his coffee and bagel at the local coffee shop and was about to cross the boulevard when he saw her. Perhaps it was the red coat or maybe the way her shiny black hair swung as she walked, but something caught his eye. He turned and watched her as she ran across the street pulling a cart stacked with files. A deputy attorney general, he decided. They were the only ones around here who hauled around stacks of files on cheap aluminum two-wheeled carts. He wondered which courtroom she might be headed for. She was new to him and he thought he'd identified all of the young D.A.G.s who worked in the family court. In any case, she was cute, and he wondered where she was headed.

Lily Hanson hurried across the street, certain she was about to be late on the first day in her new assignment.

She wasn't a new D.A.G. It was going on three years now, but she'd just been transferred from one of the suburban counties to Paterson. She would be replacing Alice Manley, who'd had a hysterical fit last Friday, and said if they didn't transfer her, she would first have a nervous breakdown and then quit. Alice also implied that she might sue the state, or at least make such a federal case out of her grievance that the papers would pick it up. Ordinarily the section chief might have balked at this obvious threat, but these were difficult times. The state of New Jersey, which paid their salaries, had a hiring freeze and the work was coming over the rafters. The federal government had recently decided to focus on child abuse, creating new laws and new regulations. Although the lawmakers may have been well intentioned, Lily wasn't so sure the new laws protected the children any better than the old ones, but she was certain that the new regulations made everyone's job even more difficult. So there was more work, but not more money, and if anyone quit he or she was not replaced. The section chief was at her wit's end and lately tended to give in to all threats, no matter how ridiculous, to keep attorneys from quitting.

All this had meant that Lily was up most of the night reviewing the cases that were scheduled for that day since she had not known about the change in assignment until the day before. Fortunately, she had enough experience to be familiar with the issues. Even so, there were twenty files and it had taken her most of the night to review them.

Lily entered the courthouse and flashed the badge that

enabled her to skirt security. She wondered for the umpteenth time what she was getting herself into. She had yet to meet her new judge or the caseworkers she would be representing in her new assignment. She'd heard the office had its share of characters and that the judge who was assigned to that office was a stickler for time. But he also had a reputation for making good decisions. She glanced at the clock as she stood in front of the elevator waiting for it to arrive. It was five to nine and she'd been told that he called the cases promptly at nine. Not a good way to begin.

When the elevator finally arrived she pushed her way to the front of the crowd, dragging her cart full of cases behind her. To heck with civility, she had to get up there. She punched in the floor and impatiently waited as the elevator slowly made its way up. By the time she got to the floor, it was just nine o'clock and she still had to figure out which courtroom was hers, and then manage to slip in unnoticed—no mean task with this box of cases. Moments later, when she was in front of the double doors marked with Judge Philip Keegan's name, she slowly opened one door and poked her head in. Keegan was on the bench and had already started. Head held high, cart behind her, red coat open but still on, she walked in and looked up. Not surprisingly Judge Keegan was staring straight at her, though his only acknowledgment was to raise one bushy eyebrow. Then he continued with the calendar call. Lily stopped in her tracks and quickly pulled out her copy of the day's court calendar. She let out a sigh and started breathing for the first time since she'd entered the courtroom when she saw that he was only on the first case on the list.

"State versus Montville," he barked.

"The state's ready, Your Honor," she loudly responded and was relieved to see the judge nod in her direction. They continued with the calendar call, him announcing, her responding (since she represented the plaintiff, the state of New Jersey, on all the cases), and any parties that were represented by lawyers also putting in their appearances as the judge quickly went down the list of cases scheduled to be heard that day. When he was finished, he motioned for her to approach. She walked up to where he was seated behind the five-foot-high bench, glad that she was, in heels, five-foot-nine tall. It was bad enough to be new and a bit frazzled, but at least she didn't have the disadvantage of not being tall enough to see over the bench and meet the judge eye to eye.

"You the new D.A.G.?"

She nodded. "Lily Hanson, Your Honor," she said, wondering if she should extend her hand. She decided against it. It would be too awkward to reach up and across.

"Alice couldn't take it anymore?"

She shrugged, wondering if it would be okay to chuckle. She decided no. "So it appears. Should I be nervous?"

Suddenly he smiled.

So he was human; she felt much better.

"You'll be all right," he said. "Though next time get here five minutes earlier."

Much to her annoyance, she could feel her face heat up. So much for being cool; her blushing always gave her away. "I'll do my best," she said. She retreated to her stack of files and set up for the day at the counsel's table. As the state's attorney, she would be required to present the facts in each case and the state's position. Best she get started. She had also heard that Judge Keegan didn't like to waste time.

Michael Frascato watched their exchange from the side of the courtroom where he did the job of the bailiff and court office: calling cases and keeping order along with protecting the judge and the rest of the participants from danger.

So the new D.A.G. had been assigned to them. He studied her, speculating. Although she was flustered, she didn't let the judge's gruff manner throw her. That was good. Alice had been too timid and had sometimes been cowed by the judge's acerbic manner, not understanding that he was just seeing if he could get her goat. Having Ms. Lily Hanson in the courtroom might make this job more interesting. At the very least, she was pleasant to look at and if she was already catching on to the judge and his ways, it might even be fun.

Chapter Two

The judge took a brief recess that gave Lily the opportunity to organize the day's files in the order they would be heard. A young dark-haired woman about her age came over and extended her hand.

"Maria Velez," she said, shaking Lily's hand. "I understand you're the new D.A.G."

Lily nodded. "You must be the law guardian," she said, meaning the public defender's appointed counsel for the child. In every family court case there was a lawyer from Lily's office representing the Division of Youth and Family Services (DYFS) and a lawyer for the child. Parents were also represented, usually by court-appointed lawyers, when they couldn't afford to hire private counsel on their own.

Maria, as the child's advocate, sat with Lily at one end of the table and the parents and their lawyers sat at the other end. Standing next to Maria, Lily could see that she was tiny—a good eight inches shorter than Lily—and very petite, except for large, heavily lashed dark brown eyes. Lily noticed that she had a slight lilt to her English and figured she'd find out later where she came from, though she suspected one of the Caribbean islands.

"Welcome to Paterson," said Maria. "I hope you enjoy it here."

"Thanks," said Lily. "I hear he"—she pointed to the bench where the judge had been sitting—"is okay to appear before."

Maria nodded. "You'll like him," she predicted, "as long as you take what he says with a grain of salt. His bark is worse than his bite. And, for the most part, his staff is great."

Lily was relieved to hear what Maria had to say and was happy to find Maria so friendly. She suspected that the woman was, like herself, somewhere in her late twenties and figured that would mean they'd have something in common and be able to connect. Life was much simpler if she could relate to the other lawyers that she dealt with.

She continued to look around as she set up her cases for the day. Seated next to the judge was his clerk who controlled the calendar. Right now the young voluptuous and attractive bottle blonde had her back to the courtroom and was immersed in a game of solitaire on the computer. Perhaps sensing that she was being studied, she looked up from her game and turned and smiled at Lily, who returned her smile.

"That's Tracy," said Maria, following her glance. She lowered her voice. "She's a real pip." She lowered it even further. "I suggest you stay on her good side if you want to get to the judge. Great kid, but if she doesn't like you she manages to lose messages and put you on the wrong side of His Honor. She's also a first-class gossip."

"Tracy, meet Lily," said Maria, speaking louder so she would be heard. "She's new, so we're going to be nice to her, at least for this week."

"I'm always nice," said Tracy, her accent immediately giving away her Jersey roots. She laughed. "Except when someone's a jerk or crosses me." She smiled sweetly at Lily. "But you don't seem the type to do that."

Although the judge had not yet come back from his chambers the defense counselors on the first case were already in their places. Lily looked over to see if she knew either of them. She didn't, but she'd been pleased to recognize a few lawyers when she'd first walked in. Any familiar face at this point was a comfort. She glanced up at the sheriff who was talking to Tracy. She was glad to see he was in terrific shape and that he was young, not much older than she. In her last assignment the sheriff had been middle-aged and overweight. She had nothing against overweight middle-aged males, except when she felt threatened or in danger in the courtroom. That did occasionally happen and Lily was glad that at least there would be some protection. This sheriff was a hunk, with piercing blue eyes and a nice smile, she'd noticed, though she'd yet to be the recipient of it.

"All rise," the sheriff suddenly barked, signaling the fact that the judge was returning to the bench. She took a deep breath. Her first day on the new assignment was officially to begin.

The sheriff called the case and swore in the parents who were present. They were sitting on the other side of the room from Maria and Lily with their lawyers. This was a straightforward case of a mother leaving her three younger children with their nine-year-old brother while she ran to the grocery store before work. The nine-year-old got frightened when it started to thunder and called the police, who in turn called the child abuse agency that Lily represented. In New Jersey, parents weren't supposed to leave kids under twelve home alone. Lily explained to the court that the parents had been very cooperative, had since taken parenting classes, and at that point seemed to understand that they should not leave their children alone, even for a few minutes to run an errand. The DYFS had already returned the kids to their parents and just wanted to keep the case open for one more review to make sure everything was okay before dismissing it. The law guardian agreed with the plan as did the judge. However, before moving on to the next case, the judge spent some time admonishing the parents about the harm that might have come to the children. A new date was set and the next case, *State v. Romano*, was called.

This case was more serious and unfortunately more

typical of the caseload. From the report that Lily had read the night before she'd learned that the children's father, Mr. Romano, regularly beat his wife and his two children, a boy and a girl. But Mrs. Romano had never told anyone. It was only when the oldest child, Justin, had gone to school with welts on his arms and legs that the matter was reported to the authorities. Mr. Romano was arrested and remained incarcerated. That day he was present in the courtroom in an orange prison suit, handcuffed and accompanied by two guards.

"Ms. Hanson," said the judge, "what's the status here?"

"Mr. Romano is scheduled to be sentenced next week. Mrs. Romano is attending therapy as ordered by the court and the children are too. We're asking that Mrs. Romano continue with her therapy so that she learns to stand up to her husband. We also ask that he be barred from the home until we have an expert's report saying that he is no longer a danger to these children and his wife."

The judge nodded. "Was that recommended by the psychologist that evaluated him?"

"Yes, Your Honor."

Ordinarily that should have been the end of it since everyone was in agreement that the mother needed to stay in therapy, but her lawyer, a man named Joe Schwinn, whom Lily knew by reputation, wanted to have his say and when he did, he went on at length describing how much work his client had done and how much of a victim she had been. At first Lily paid attention, but when he started to repeat himself, she began to look around the courtroom, finally relaxed enough to take in her surroundings. The judge appeared to be listening and was writing furiously. Lily couldn't help wondering if what he was writing had anything to do with what the mother's lawyer was saying. Tracy had her back to the room and was working at the computer. It took only one swing of her chair for Lily to see that she was back to her game of solitaire. Maria was doodling, and Lily was about to do the same when she looked over at the sheriff and discovered that he was watching her with what could only be described as amusement. Without thinking, Lily rolled her eyes. The sheriff's mouth twitched as if he was trying to keep himself from smiling. Lily looked down at her notes. It wouldn't do to get caught looking unprofessional—at least on her first day.

The morning sped by. Except when Joe Schwinn was involved, the pace was brisk and the judge did not spend a lot of time giving his opinion. Maria was also succinct so they got through more than half the cases by the time they took a break for lunch at one. When they came back in the afternoon, there were only five cases left. Unfortunately, one involved Joe Schwinn and went on for an hour. This time Schwinn even complimented Lily, saying that already it was clear that her capable lawyering was going to be of great benefit to Passaic County. This time Lily didn't dare to look the sheriff's way for fear she would laugh out loud. It had been a long day and any restraint she might have had was gone. Finally they finished the calendar at four thirty.

"How about going out for a beer to celebrate your first day?" said Maria. "You did great."

"A beer sounds good," said Lily. It would give her a chance to get to know Maria a little better and she did feel like celebrating. Beginnings were never easy. Besides, it was Friday afternoon and she had no place to rush off to.

Mulcahy's, just around the corner from the courthouse, was a typical Irish pub with sawdust on the worn wooden floor, a tin-plated ceiling, and a long, shiny wooden bar with brass railing taking up most of the interior. The bar was jammed. Lily scanned the crowd as she followed Maria inside. There were far more men than women. She also noted that the crowd was a real mix of what must go on in the neighborhood. While the women were mostly dressed in suits and were probably lawyers and court personnel, the men were more diverse. Lots of suits, many she took to be lawyers, and a good number of more casually attired males. Some, by their short hair, broad chests, and wide-legged stances she pegged as cops and some, by their sun-worn faces, were obviously construction workers. Others she wasn't so sure about. With casual Friday becoming more common they could easily be from the surrounding office buildings. Maria spotted two stools together and signaled for Lily to follow her.

"I'll buy," Maria said, settling in to her seat. "Quick, make up your mind before Terry comes over," she said, nodding in the direction of the bartender. "He doesn't have a lot of patience."

Lily picked one of the beers they had on draft and after they gave their order, Maria turned to her.

"So tell me about yourself," she said. "Married, kids, boyfriend?"

Lily grinned. "Not married, no kids, but I do have a boyfriend."

Maria nodded. "So what's his deal? Is he a lawyer too?"

Lily shook her head. "He's a doctor. He just finished his surgical residency."

Maria nodded. "Very impressive. Does that mean you two are going to start thinking about something permanent?"

Lily smiled at her new friend's bluntness and shook her head. "That sounds like a question my mother would ask, particularly to someone our age." She paused and took a sip of the beer that had been placed before her. "No commitment. Not right now. He isn't even around. He's working out in South Dakota."

Maria shook her head and took a swallow of her beer. "Wow! That's not terribly convenient. What's he doing out there? Family?"

"No, he's working on an Indian reservation. It's a program they have where they volunteer in places where there aren't enough doctors and the people don't have any medical care."

Maria nodded sympathetically. "It's great that he does it, but tough on you, huh?"

Lily nodded. "I guess, but I'm kind of used to it. We haven't been living in the same city since college. He went to med school in Boston and I was in law school in New York."

Maria shook her head. "Was that on purpose?"

"Not really," said Lily. She paused and took another sip, enjoying the cold sensation as it ran down her throat. "It just worked out that way. But we also made a point of doing what we thought was best for our careers. We figured if our relationship was any good it would weather the separation." That's what Josh always said, anyway. Sometimes Lily wondered if always being separated put an unnatural strain on the relationship and made life overly difficult. But she never said that to Josh. He'd say she was being shortsighted and insensitive, particularly when it came to his career and the sacrifices he was making.

"So tell me," Maria asked Lily, "what's 'our' age?" She grinned to soften the question.

"Twenty-seven?" said Lily. "That's how old I am."

Maria nodded. "Twenty-nine. I'll be thirty next February."

"So what about you?" asked Lily. "Single? Married? Kids? Anyone significant?"

"One little girl, Isabelle, no husband." Maria paused and took a swallow of her beer. "And there is someone significant, though I can't figure out how significant." She looked over at Lily and sighed. "Kind of hard when you have a kid. Not every man likes them—especially when he wants to be romantic."

"What about Isabelle's father?"

"It didn't work out. Never should have been involved. But then along came Isabelle and I have never regretted her. I had her when I was in law school. Fortunately my mother has always been around to help me. That's where Isabelle is right now. I'll pick her up on my way home and by that time my mother will have already given her dinner." She took a long sip of her beer and put down the mug. "Don't get me wrong, I'm not against getting married again, but Isabelle and I do okay on our own."

"There is a gentleman on the other side of the bar who wants to buy you lovely ladies a beer. Will you oblige him?" Terry smiled and winked at them both.

Maria grinned and nodded.

"Who is it?" asked Lily.

Maria pointed to the other side where Michael, the sheriff in Judge Keegan's courtroom, was sitting with several other sheriffs. He smiled and nodded when they looked over. "Thanks," called Maria. "Very generous."

Before Lily had a chance to ask Maria about him, he was headed over to them.

"Michael Frascato," he said when he reached her, extending his hand. "Welcome to Paterson. How are you liking it so far?"

"Thanks for the drink," said Lily, shaking his hand. "So far I do. You've all been very welcoming today."

Michael grinned. "I don't know about that. You got a good cross section of the characters though, including Joe Schwinn. I sometimes think he gets paid by the word." He looked over at Maria. "And Tracy was on good behavior. The judge probably told her not to scare you off, at least not on the first day." He looked up at the clock that was hanging on the wall and sighed. "Unfortunately duty calls and I've got to get going. Enjoy the weekend," he said. "I'll see you guys next week."

Maria glanced over at Lily as Michael walked off. "He's a cutie pie, huh?"

Lily nodded and grinned. "I noticed."

"He's also a good guy, which can be a real plus in that courtroom, particularly when it comes to trouble-makers.

Chapter Three

On her way home, Lily stopped and picked up salad ingredients for dinner at the farmers' market near her apartment. Even though it was Friday night, traditionally the time to go out and party, she and her roommates had agreed they'd stay in and spend their last night home together. Both her roommates were moving out by the end of the weekend.

She walked into the apartment and bit back the words of frustration that had immediately come to her lips. The living room was a disaster. Half-filled boxes were everywhere. Clothes were piled on every single chair and closet doors were ajar with shoes and coats mixed together in piles around the not-very-big room. Although she would be sorry to see her roommates go, part of her was looking forward to it. At least the chaos would be gone.

But Lily still hadn't figured out where she was going

to live. This impending move had happened suddenly and she still hadn't completely adjusted her thinking to the change. Jessica, whom Lily had known since college—and the initial reason that Lily had moved to New Jersey—had come home the weekend before, announcing her engagement to Seth and saying she was moving to Boston to be with him. Seth was coming down that weekend to help her move up there. Around the same time, their roommate Arlene was accepted into grad school and decided to move home to save money until school started. Her dad was coming in on Sunday to help her move out, so she'd also be gone before the end of the weekend.

Lily wasn't ready for all this to be happening. She liked things just the way they were, but it looked like she had no choice. Josh had another year in South Dakota and she had no plans to change her job. She couldn't afford the apartment by herself so she had two weeks to find another apartment close enough to work that she could afford on a D.A.G. salary.

She hadn't focused on the move because of her new assignment, and in some ways she'd been glad for the distraction. It had kept her mind off her relationship with Josh, the distance between them, and the weekend before when she'd gone out to South Dakota for a weekend rendezvous. The weekend had been less than perfect. She kept telling herself it was natural for her and Josh to sometimes get irritated or bored with each other, but lately she'd begun to feel as if the fun was slowly leaking out of their relationship. The last time she'd been out there, two weeks before, it had been particularly bad. Josh had to work most of weekend and when he wasn't working he was tired and distracted. She got irritated, he got defensive, then he apologized and she felt guilty. He was, after all, a doctor, saving lives. How could she resent the fact that he focused on his patients instead of on her all the time? They went round and round like that all weekend until it was time for her to go home.

When they'd first started dating, six years earlier, every time they'd been together, no matter what they were doing, it had been fun. When they were together, they often got silly and there were times when they'd do nothing but laugh. But even when they weren't laughing, they had a lot to talk about. A sigh slipped out as she reached down to pick up a coat that had fallen off the pile on the chair. Those good times seemed like such a long time ago. Maybe it was inevitable that some of the fun and romance would fade. Josh worked long hours and when they did see each other, which wasn't very often, one of them had just gotten off an airplane and was suffering from jet lag. She sighed again, squeezing past a stack of boxes to get through to the kitchen. They'd promised each other that their love could stand the test of time and distance. She gritted her teeth with determination. She wasn't about to wimp out and say that it hadn't been strong enough. Instead, she decided, if fun was what she wanted, then it was up to her to make sure there was fun when she was with Josh.

But no matter what was going on with her and Josh, she needed someplace to live. Now that the weekend had finally come she planned to do some serious thinking as she walked through prospective neighborhoods. Her apartment was in Hoboken, but the rents there were stiff for one person. If Lily wanted to live alone, and she was thinking that she did, she'd have to look elsewhere. Although Newark was beginning a renaissance, she had decided that the most likely option would be Jersey City. But she didn't really know Jersey City and would have to spend this weekend trying to figure out the neighborhoods and decide which one would work for her.

"Anybody home?" she called as she walked into the kitchen. She surveyed it with dismay. Someone had started to unload dishes from the cabinets and then stopped midstream. Pots and pans were stacked on the kitchen table and glasses lined the edge of the sink. It didn't look like any dinner was going to be cooked there tonight. Pizza or Chinese would have to do and they'd probably have to eat it standing up.

"Sorry about the mess," said Jessica, walking into the kitchen. "I can put the dishes back if you want. I started to pack the stuff when I remembered—"

Lily shook her head. "It doesn't matter. Why don't we just order in? I can eat this some other time," she added, indicating the salad greens she'd bought at the market. "There's no sense in making dinner more complicated than it needs to be." She opened the fridge and put the greens on one of the empty shelves. "Better yet, we should just go out." She looked back at Jessica. "Where's Arlene?"

"She called and said she'd be home by seven," said Jessica, glancing at her watch, "so that should be any minute. She left about an hour ago with a bunch of boxes to bring home to her parents'."

Dinner at their favorite Italian joint was fun if not a bit melancholy. Lily sensed that at least Jessica had already moved on. She looked over at Lily at one point during dinner. "Did you ever consider moving out to South Dakota so you could be with Josh?"

Lily shook her head after taking a sip of her wine. She'd suggested that to Josh a while back, but he'd said no. Not sensible, he'd said. They only had another year. "We talked about that, but it doesn't make any sense," she explained to her friends. "There are no jobs out there and ultimately Josh plans to work on the East Coast, probably New York. This is the time for me to start my career here. It's only for another year or so. We can wait." She hoped she sounded more hopeful than she felt. It was a passing slump, she was sure, but as she glanced down at Jessica's sparkling diamond, she couldn't help but feel a little bit envious. "It's not that I don't ever want to be married," she added, "but Josh feels very strongly that he needs to be established before we take that step."

"Well, you're lucky he's so sensible," said Arlene, refilling her glass. "Better that than some macho guy who talks big but can't deliver. You should see what's out there! Pickings aren't great. Believe me!"

Lily did. Arlene had brought home many of the pickings and each time she did Lily thanked her lucky stars for Josh. Of course she never said that to Arlene, but silently agreed every time Arlene made a comment about all the good guys being taken once you reach a certain age.

"What about your job?" asked Jessica. "Any chance you might make a move? Join me in Boston?"

Lily shook her head. Josh was thinking New York would be a good place to practice, so moving to Boston made no sense. Besides, she liked her job. She didn't really want to move, unless it meant being with Josh. "I never expected to get attached to Jersey but now that I'm here, I kind of like it," she explained.

"Your new assignment looks okay?"

She nodded. She really did think she was going to like being in Paterson, as crazy as that sounded. For the first time in a long time, she felt as if something fit just right.

By Sunday night Lily was alone. Her roommates had left in two waves. Jessica's fiancé, Seth, had picked her up around noon, loading up a U-Haul with her belongings. Arlene had left in the late afternoon. Her father had come to load up the big stuff like her mattress and couch earlier that afternoon. She'd promised to come back at seven to have a final dinner with Lily.

"I'll be fine, really," said Lily as they parted in front of the restaurant. "I just have to figure out where to live." She gave Arlene a hug. "It's not like we won't be seeing each other, you know. You're only in the next county."

Arlene grinned and nodded. "I'm probably projecting. After all, I'm the one who is going home to Mom and Dad. I hope I'm not making a mistake."

Lily shook her head. "You're just being sensible.

This way you'll be able to afford a place in New York when you're in grad school. It's the best decision for you." That was true, but Lily was also realizing that she was excited at the prospect of being on her own for the first time.

Lily had spent Saturday walking around Jersey City trying to figure out where she should live. Even though she'd been in New Jersey since she finished law school, Jersey City was still an unknown. She and her roommates had lived in Hoboken and if they didn't go out there, they took the PATH into New York. Lily had talked to a few real estate agents and a handful of people in her office who lived in Jersey City, so she knew what neighborhoods to look at. But before she committed, she wanted to get a feel for the place.

Jersey City was much bigger than Hoboken and she soon discovered that getting to know it was going to be more difficult than she had imagined. There were many new buildings along the waterfront that had great views of Manhattan and the Hudson River. Heading west, into the interior of the city, there were brownstones and low apartment buildings on tree-lined streets. Beyond that were huge expanses of apartment buildings where Lily imagined families lived. There also were pockets of poverty scattered throughout. It was a typical, industrial Northeast city. After stopping to talk to rental agents in several of the high-rises along the river and walking the streets of the two neighborhoods that she'd targeted as suitable for a young single woman, she decided that a brownstone in one of the tree-lined neighborhoods, near a park, would be her first choice. By that time it was five o'clock and already dusk. She didn't have a lot of time before her lease ran out but she'd have to wait until the following week to look again. She comforted herself with the fact that she'd at least narrowed down her search.

Chapter Four

Lily was in court again on Tuesday. The new assignment had begun to feel more comfortable. She was starting to know what to expect from Judge Keegan; what would set him off; what would placate him; and what would amuse him. Lily prided herself on being able to make anyone laugh and Judge Keegan was no exception. She also knew from experience that it helped to have a sense of humor when the cases got tough. Not that there was anything funny about child abuse or neglect, but she found that if she didn't find the humor in the human situation, she was lost.

Maria Velez, the court-appointed lawyer for the children, continued to be a pleasure to work with and, as she suspected, one of the public defenders, Joe Schwinn, was proving to be such a pompous windbag that there were times she had trouble keeping a straight face when he was on his feet. It usually occurred when she happened to catch Michael's eye, which seemed to be happening quite a lot. On one case, Schwinn had spent five minutes praising the judge for his cogent rulings and another five applauding the American way. When he started in on the wonders of democracy, she caught Michael making a face. Then their eyes met briefly with understanding before Lily looked down to keep from laughing or doing something equally inappropriate.

The first case on the calendar that morning involved three teenage boys. Their mother was a drug addict and out on the streets; their dads (each had a different one) were missing. The boys lived with their grandmother. Throughout the history of the case, the big issue had been adequate housing, always a problem in the inner city. However, today they were in court because of school attendance, or the lack thereof. The boys preferred going into New York City to attending middle school in Paterson, and their grandmother had trouble stopping them. Lily had asked for an emergent hearing as a last resort, hoping that the judge could scare the boys into going to school.

Michael went out into the hall and called the case. Ms. Wenzel, the boys' grandmother, and the three boys, Tim, Todd, and Tucker, shuffled in. Lily looked over at them, curious since she'd never seen them before. She was new to the case, but had reviewed their file before coming to court. The boys had a long history of mischief and truancy that had only gotten worse as they got older.

They looked younger than she expected and, at the moment, were obviously scared. Lily's intention was to take advantage of that fear. She began the hearing by explaining to the court that the boys had not been going to school. She continued by telling the judge about their selling candy on the subways in New York City. While not characterizing the selling of candy as high crimes and misdemeanors, she did express the attorney general's grave concern over their truancy. The judge nodded somberly and then focused on Tim, the oldest of the three.

"Tim," he said, his deep voice resonating in the courtroom, "how old are you?"

"Fourteen," said Tim, his voice barely audible.

"Is it true you don't go to school every day?"

The boy nodded.

"Speak up," said Judge Keegan. "This hearing is being recorded. Do you know what that means?"

"I think so," squeaked Tim.

Keegan explained anyway. "We're making a record of this hearing so that we can go back and look at it later if we need to. You understand?"

"Uh-huh."

"Good. Now back to your going to school, or from what Ms. Hanson's telling me, not going to school. How did you do last year?"

Tim shrugged. "Okay."

"Did you get promoted?"

"No."

"You didn't. So what grade are you in?"

"Seventh."

"And you should be in the eighth?"

"Uh-huh."

"So instead of going to school, you go into New York and sell candy."

"Uh-huh."

"And you bring your younger brothers along."

"Yeah."

"Where do you get the candy?"

"There's a guy I know. It's his older brother. He gets it for us."

"And you pay him for it?"

"Yeah."

"How much money do you make after you pay him?"

Tim paused for a moment, seeming to be doing some calculations. "About ten cents a bar."

"And you skip school and take your brothers into New York to do this?"

"Yeah."

"Anybody tell you about the youth house?"

"Yeah," his voice suddenly almost inaudible.

"Do you like living with your grandmother and your brothers?"

"Yeah."

"What do you think I should do? You've already missed"—the judge checked the sheet in front of him—"twenty days of school this year. That alone is enough reason to send you away. Is that what you want?"

The boy shook his head.

"Speak up."

"No. That's not what I want."

"What should we do?" asked the judge.

"Leave me with my brothers and my grandma."

"What about school?"

"I'll go."

"How often?"

"Every day."

"How do I know that?"

"I promise." By now Tim was crying. Lily could see the tears running down his face when she looked over, in spite of his putting his head down. His brothers stood on either side of him also crying and his grandmother looked as if she was on the verge of doing so.

The judge addressed Lily. "Well, Ms. Hanson. What do you think?"

Lily shrugged and tried to sound stern. "I may regret this, but I say give him one more chance. If Tim really goes to school we won't ask for his removal. But if he misses any days at all we will come back to court immediately, we will ask you to order Tim's removal and for him to be placed in the youth house until a more appropriate place can be found for him."

The judge nodded and then turned to Maria. "Ms. Velez?"

"I concur with the attorney general. If Tim does not go to school we do not want him to remain with his brothers because he is a bad influence on them."

"Do you understand what everyone is saying?" the judge asked Tim.

"Yes, sir."

"Very good. Remember, we're counting on you." He turned to Lily. "What do you say we bring this case back in three months unless Tim does not go to school?"

The matter was concluded and Michael led the family out and called the next case on the calendar.

"Scared the dickens out of that kid," said Michael as he walked by Lily while the next case was being set up."

"I hope so," she said.

"Okay if I signed them up for my basketball league?" Both Maria and Lily looked up. "Basketball league?"

"Yeah." He nodded. "I run a league," he said, "at night, after work. We've got a bunch of high school boys that I and some of the other sheriffs have formed into teams. We play most of the year—a couple of nights a week."

Lily looked over at Maria. "Any objection?"

She shook her head. "Can't think of one. In fact I think it sounds wonderful. Can I get you to take a couple of other kids?"

He shrugged. "No problem. That's what it's for."

What a terrific idea, thought Lily, and so obvious. These sheriffs wouldn't be intimidated by these street kids and would be able to talk to them.

When the judge took a short recess, Lily and Maria asked Michael more about the league. He gave them the details: practice two nights a week and games on Saturday mornings and a number to call. Then he went off to check in the prisoners, two dead-beat dads, who would be coming up on the next case.

While they waited, Lily told Maria about her housing crisis. "I've got to find something by the end of the month," she said, explaining how she'd narrowed the search down to Jersey City. "Manhattan and Hoboken are too expensive if I want to live alone, but I don't know where to begin looking."

She didn't have a chance to get into very much because the judge came back on the bench and the next case was called.

At lunchtime Maria took Lily to one of Paterson's premier pizza joints in the nearby Italian section of the city. Even though the ambiance left something to be desired, the tiled floors and Formica-covered tables were a little worn and the fluorescent lighting was not flattering, the pizza was the best Lily had ever had and the price was right. While they ate, Maria told Lily about her weekend, explaining that her boyfriend Joe wanted to marry her.

"I'm just not sure," said Maria, taking a bite of her pizza. "I'm managing fine on my own," she continued after swallowing.

"How's he with your daughter?" asked Lily, sipping her soda.

"He's great with her."

"And you love him?" Lily asked after cutting another piece and putting it on her plate.

"Sure. Absolutely."

Lily shrugged. "A lot of women would jump at the chance."

Maria grimaced. "I know. Maybe I'm being stupid. I just don't know if I want to risk it."

"How's Joe about your hesitation?"

"Fine for now, but I don't think he's going to be

patient forever. He'd like to settle down and have a family." She shook her head. "Maybe it's what I want too. I just don't know."

It was at the end of the court day that Michael approached Lily. "Understand you're looking for a place in Jersey City."

Lily was signing off on the completed court orders. Maria had already left to go pick up her daughter. While she packed up her files, Lily explained about her roommates and having to get out by the end of the month. "The trouble is I don't even know where to begin. I looked at some neighborhoods last weekend, but I have no sense of what things really cost or where would be right for me."

"I might be able to help," he said, arranging the chairs in front of the counselor's table and stacking the law books that had been left there.

"Really?"

"Yeah." He came over and leaned on the table where Lily had been working. "My brothers and I have a couple of buildings. Let me talk to them."

"That would be great," she said, afraid to hope that she could be lucky enough to find an apartment so easily.

"Want to give me your number? One of us will call you and let you know."

She nodded and quickly scribbled her home number on the back of one of her cards and handed it to him.

Michael called her only a few days later. "We've got one apartment that's available on Hamilton Park," he said.

"That's a great area," she said. In fact, it was the absolute best: cozy, charming, and filled with people just like herself. She knew that much about Jersey City. "But what are you asking for it? It might be too much for my budget."

Michael quoted a price.

"I could manage that," she said. "When can I see it?" She was amazed that there really was an apartment that she could afford and figured there was probably something wrong with it. Even so, it was still worth a look.

Chapter Five

Most weeks Lily spent three days in the office, one day in court, and one day with her client, the Division of Youth and Family Services. Today was an office day and she had a stack of paperwork to sort through, as well as cases to organize for the court reviews the following day. First she checked her e-mail. It was the way she communicated with her colleagues and also how she kept in touch with her friends. Besides an e-mail from Josh with some news about his family, one from her mother telling her about another of Lily's classmates getting married, and one from her brother, passing on a very funny joke, there were two e-mails of interest that morning. The first one was from Arlene. She reported that already she hated living at home even if it was for the best and the only way she'd be able to pay for grad school. But the main reason for the e-mail was to find out if Lily would join her, her new boyfriend, and his frat brother for dinner Saturday night. The fraternity brother was going to be in from Denver for the weekend and they were trying to make plans. To cement things with the boyfriend, Lily figured. It would be good to see Arlene and meet the new boyfriend, so even though Lily had been thinking she should spend the weekend walking around Jersey City since time was running short, she figured she'd do it. She e-mailed back saying she would join them.

The next e-mail was much more interesting, albeit impractical. One of the lawyers in her office was looking for a home for his dog. They had a new baby and his wife was too overwhelmed to also deal with the dog. He described the dog as a mixed breed, part retriever and part lab, a good companion, and trained, with all his shots. The problem was that the dog needed a good run several times a week and neither her colleague nor his wife had the time anymore. He concluded by saying the dog's name was Sam and invited anyone interested down to his office to see a picture of Sam. Lily got up and headed down the hall, knowing full well that a dog would be a crazy idea. She was having enough trouble finding an apartment, why make it harder by having a dog? Even as she told herself how impractical it was, she envisioned Sam and herself walking through city streets and down country lanes. She would just take a quick look. Maybe the dog would look unfriendly and she wouldn't be tempted. Her colleague's office was empty, but there was a framed picture of a beautiful golden-haired dog on the credenza along with pictures of the man with his wife and new baby. She stood staring at the picture. If she had a dog, she wouldn't be alone in her apartment. She'd have to run in the morning. She wouldn't mind spending Saturday nights staying in and watching TV. Sam would be at her side, his head in her lap.

"So what do you think?" came a voice from behind her.

Lily turned around and met the eyes of her colleague, Don Jones, Sam's owner, at least for now.

"Nice dog," she said.

He nodded. "Hate to give him up, but as I said, it's too much to expect my wife to take care of the baby and the dog and work part-time, and I'm not there enough to be much help."

"How long have you had him?"

He shrugged. "About four years. I got him when he was a puppy. I brought him to the marriage."

"I shouldn't even be talking to you. I'm in no position to take a dog. I was just curious when I saw your notice. I'm sure there are a million people here in the office who are better situated to help you out. I don't even have an apartment," she said, continuing to stare at the picture.

"I don't know about there being a million people ready to take him," said Don. "You're the first I've heard from. How about if I keep you in mind and let you know if anyone else shows any interest? If you even think that you might be interested, I could check with you before I give him away."

She shook her head. "I don't want you to do that. But if he's still around . . . ," she said, her voice trailing off.

Don grinned. "I'll keep you posted. Okay?"

She nodded. "Okay." She walked back to her office wondering what had possessed her to even have that conversation.

Late in the afternoon she got a call about the apartment.

"Michael said you were looking for a place," said the caller without introducing himself.

"Is this Michael's brother?" said Lily, quickly figuring out who it must be.

"Yeah. I'm Patrick. You interested?"

"Maybe. Michael didn't tell me much about it. Just that it was on Hamilton Park in Jersey City."

"We just finished fixing it up this week. Only bought the building a month ago and it's the first one we've completed in there. Means it would be noisy during the day. We'll be renovating the others."

"That's okay. I work during the day. So tell me about it."

"Not too much to tell. It's a one-bedroom, nice kitchen, just redone. A bath, that's new too, big windows, a little garden." He paused as if thinking. "It's safe. Good neighborhood. I'd let my sister live there."

Lily could feel herself bristle and before she knew it the words were out. "Really? You'd *let* your sister, huh?"

There was a heavy sigh. "I should let Michael do the talking. He's the smooth one in the family. I always put my foot in my mouth. What I mean is"—he cleared his throat—"it's safe."

"Sounds fine," she said, backing off. Fact was Patrick sounded sweet and she was mad at herself for taking offense at his paternalism. He obviously was just trying to be a good guy. "Can I see it after work?"

"Tonight?" He seemed startled at her request.

"Or some other night this week. Whatever works for you."

"Can't do it tonight. How about tomorrow? One of us can be around tomorrow."

"That's fine," said Lily. "About six?"

"Yeah, six is good."

"Okay. Oh, by the way, what's your policy on pets?" She couldn't believe she'd just asked that.

"Policy? Pets?" He paused and there was a long silence. "I don't know about any policy. Let me check with Michael. Maybe he knows about our policy. Okay? See you about six. And we'll tell you the policy then."

She had court the next day. "I'm seeing that apartment tonight," she said when she saw Michael.

He grinned. "I know. And you gave my brother the business."

She could feel herself redden. "You mean about 'letting' his sister live there? I didn't mean to. It just came out."

"I figured." He continued to smile, seeming to be amused about something. Lily found herself feeling off center and she didn't like it. What did she care what Michael and his brother thought: as long as she was a good tenant and even then only if she liked the apartment.

Michael arched an eyebrow. "Got a dog?"

She shook her head and didn't meet his eyes. "He said he'd check with you—"

"About our policy," Michael said, still looking amused. "What kind of dog?"

She sighed. "It's someone in the office. They've got a dog that needs a home." She explained about Sam.

Michael shrugged. "Pat tell you that they'll be working in the building during the day?"

She nodded.

"If it doesn't bother the dog, we don't mind. There's the park right there where you can walk him."

"I don't have him," she said feeling kind of silly. "I just wondered."

At the next break Michael came by the counsel table. "I just talked to Pat. I'll bring you over after work. Okay?"

"I've got my car."

"That's fine. You can follow me."

"Excuse me."

Lily and Michael both looked up to see Tracy standing there. Lily hadn't noticed that she was still in the room or she would have been more careful.

"So you're renting Michael's apartment?" she asked, pushing her blond curls out of her eyes in such a way that she managed to reveal even more of her ample chest.

Lily shook her head, wondering what had ever possessed her to have a personal conversation in the courtroom. Tracy missed nothing. "I don't know yet. I'm seeing it tonight," she admitted.

"My fiancé and I got a place up in North Bergen, right on the river. He's living there until we get married," she said. "My parents would kill me if I moved in with him," she looked around to see who was in the courtroom as she spoke.

"So have you set a date?" asked Maria, who had just arrived.

Tracy nodded. "Next year, August 12. Got the place and everything. Only thing left is the band. We're going out this Saturday to listen to three." She looked down at the diamond on her finger and sighed, "It's not easy to plan a wedding and work too."

The judge walked in and they all rose from their seats. Lily would have to wait to hear about the rest of Tracy's wedding plans.

At the end of the day Michael was waiting for her, hanging out by the counsel table as she finished her orders. "I'll give you a hand with that cart," he said, eyeing the ungainly boxes stacked precariously on the metal wagon.

Lily smiled and shook her head. "You don't have to. I'm used to managing it."

"Nah. My mother would not be happy with me if she heard I didn't offer a hand," he said smiling. "Where are you parked?"

Michael explained that his car was parked in the basement of the building. Lily's was across the street in the municipal lot. "I'll walk over with you," he said, "and give you directions to the house in case you get lost."

She nodded. Getting lost seemed like a very real possibility. She had enough trouble finding her way around Paterson, but Jersey City seemed like a real puzzle.

But Michael was easy to follow, at least partially because he drove a red Jeep, which was simple to spot on the highway even when he was a few cars ahead of her. In half an hour they were making their way through the side streets of Jersey City and it wasn't long after that they pulled into a square with a park in the center, surrounded on all sides by brownstones. They pulled up in front of one of the houses behind a battered pickup truck. A man immediately leaped out of the front seat of the truck.

Lily grinned when she saw him. Rarely had she seen two brothers look more alike. Like Michael, Patrick was tall and good-looking and built like a linebacker. Observing them standing there side by side, they looked like two powerful bulls with their broad, muscular shoulders and wide backs and chests, even more apparent on Patrick because he wore a red plaid lumber jacket that accentuated it. The jeans weren't by any designer, just plain old-fashioned wranglers. But they fit him well and made Lily wonder what Michael might look like when he wasn't in his boxy sheriff's uniform. She banished that thought as soon as it reared its inappropriate head. She'd promised herself when she started law school that she would never mix business and pleasure. The promise had served her well so far and she intended to keep it. Besides, she already had a boyfriend, didn't she?

She watched as the two brothers greeted each other

affectionately, shaking hands and grabbing each other around the neck. She was fascinated. Her two brothers would no more have greeted each other with such tenderness than kiss each other on the lips. Maybe it was the Italian thing, she decided. WASPs were not exactly noted for their warmth, though she hoped she herself was an exception to that stereotype.

Michael introduced his brother who, Lily noticed, gave her a thorough once-over. Was there some attractiveness requirement to renting the apartment? She was tempted to ask, but thought better of it. She'd already put her foot in her mouth once. She didn't want to alienate him before she even had a chance to see the apartment. Instead she extended her hand and greeted him. "So which building?" she said. "I'm very curious to see the apartment."

Patrick pointed to the building that they were standing in front of. "The apartment that's available is on the ground floor," he explained. They followed him to the door that was just to the left of the front steps. There was a wrought-iron door over a wooden one. He unlocked both and motioned for them to follow him inside. The first thing Lily noticed was the smell of fresh paint as she followed Patrick and Michael down a narrow passage that opened up to a large living room. At the end of the room was a large sliding-glass door leading into a small, walled-in garden flooded with sunshine. Lily was immediately enchanted, already envisioning her furniture in the room and herself out in the garden watering flowers and herbs. Even in the late afternoon, the room was bright, probably because of the large window at the back and the fact that it was a southwest exposure. The garden walls were covered in vines and Lily knew enough about construction, as one of her brothers was a contractor, to know that the renovation that Patrick had done was first class. However, instead of telling the brothers that this was far more than she could ever have hoped for, she just nodded, almost afraid to be too enthusiastic, lest they change their minds and raise the rent or give it to someone else.

"We put a special bolt on the sliding-glass door," said Patrick, "so you shouldn't have to worry about intruders."

Michael nodded. "Besides, those walls are over six feet high. Most intruders are too lazy to bother. There are easier places to rob."

She nodded still not saying anything. She wasn't worried about intruders. This neighborhood was known to be safe. She just wanted to know if she could really live here. Besides the wonderful garden the living room had a fireplace where logs had already been laid out in anticipation of a fire. It could not be more perfect and she still hadn't seen the rest of the apartment.

"The kitchen is through this door," said Patrick. "Want to take a look?"

Wordlessly, she followed him into a room with a window facing the street.

"It's real sunny in the morning," said Patrick.

She looked around the small and compact kitchen with its exposed brick walls and shiny new appliances and pictured her plants on the windowsill.

"We left a space here in the center of the room for a table," said Patrick. "You'll probably want one since there isn't too much counter space."

"Is there a washer and dryer?" asked Lily. She would have taken the place whether there was or not, but thought she should be asking questions so she didn't seem too easy.

"Right over here," said Patrick, opening a wide door behind which a washer and dryer were stacked.

Michael walked into the kitchen. He'd gone out to the back to pick up the paintbrushes that had been left there. "You like it?" he asked.

She nodded.

"Want to see the bedroom?"

When she nodded, they led her to the other side of the living room. Two doors faced each other. Patrick opened one and pointed into the bathroom, which was a small but serviceable room. It obviously had just been done over. The bathroom even had a little window, another place for a plant. Patrick opened the other door to the bedroom, which was also small, but just fine. Lily quickly looked around long enough to confirm that it would fit her queen-size bed and a dresser. Then she noticed a folding door at the end of the room. She walked over and opened it to find a very large closet. She would have taken the apartment even if it had no closets, but this was heaven.

"What do I need to do to hold it?"

"Huh?"

"I'd like the apartment."

"Oh. It's yours."

She grinned. "Wonderful. When can I move in?"

Patrick shrugged. "Anytime."

"How about this weekend?"

"Fine."

"And you have a lease for me to sign? And you'll want a deposit?"

Patrick looked questioningly at Michael.

Michael looked sheepish. "I guess we should tell you that you're the first person outside of family to rent from us, so we're still new at this." He grinned. "But you're being a big help. We'll be ready for the next tenant. Right, Pat?"

"I hope so," said Patrick. He sighed. "Did you come up with a policy on pets?" he asked his brother.

"Yeah. They can't mind construction."

Patrick shrugged. "That makes sense."

These guys needed help, she thought. "Do you have a lease?" she asked.

"We must. Don't we?" Michael asked Patrick.

"We never needed one before. Ma would have had our heads if we'd made her or Uncle Tony sign leases."

"But I need to sign one and so does any other tenant that's not a relative. Actually, relatives should sign them too. Are you charging them rent?" Not that it was any of her business.

"Not Ma, but we're charging Uncle Tony."

"And nothing's in writing?"

"No."

"You have a lawyer, right?"

Neither man answered.

She sighed. "You should have a lawyer. Didn't you have one when you bought this building?"

When they didn't answer immediately she moved on. "I'll get a sample lease for you. If you want, I'll make sure your rights are covered so you can use it for other tenants. Okay?"

They nodded.

"You are renting to other people, right?"

"Yeah," said Michael. "You just happen to be the first. The other building is fully rented but it's my mother, Uncle Tony, and his daughter, my cousin Marianne. As we said, except for my mother, they're paying rent."

"Good." She wasn't sure why this wasn't important to her, but it suddenly seemed to be. "I'll get the lease, give you a copy, and after you check it out, I'll sign it. Then I'll move in. Okay?"

They both nodded.

"When do you think? Saturday?" asked Michael.

"Is that okay?"

"Sure."

There was a lot to do between Tuesday and Saturday, particularly since Lily had to work. But somehow she managed, staying up late every night, packing and sorting and organizing. By Friday night she was ready for the move. Because she didn't have much, only her bedroom furniture and a kitchen table and chairs, clothes and some hand-me-down dishes, she didn't need a regular mover. But she did need someone who could help her carry her furniture out of one apartment into the other and transport it from Hoboken to Jersey City. Fortunately, her secretary's boyfriend volunteered for the job. He even said he'd do it for free—since she was single and alone—but Lily had every intention of paying him. She also got a sample lease and gave it to Michael to look over. He returned it, saying he'd trust her to make sure it was okay, and she signed it after making him promise not to let anyone else rent without a signed lease. She also told him to get a lawyer, but she wasn't sure that he believed her when she said how important it was.

Her secretary's boyfriend arrived promptly and didn't take long to pack her things into his van. Lily led the way over to Jersey City and to the street where her new apartment was located. When she pulled up, Michael was standing in the front of the building waiting. There was a young man standing there with him.

"Meet the baby brother," said Michael. "Lily, meet Anthony."

Lily took full measure of Anthony. He looked nothing like his older brothers, being medium sized, and instead of having jet-black hair and deep blue eyes, he was blond and brown-eyed.

Anthony knocked his brother on the side of his head before extending his hand to Lily. "He's just jealous because I got all the looks," he said with a grin.

"Which he tries to convince us makes up for the height," said Michael with an easy smile.

"Well, you don't look anything like them," said Lily.

"That was always the question growing up," he said. "Who was adopted. Actually, I look like my dad, except for my height," he said, a sparkle in his eye. "When you meet my mother, you'll figure out where that comes from. And yes, my dad was Italian too. Just from the north."

"Can we give you a hand?" asked Patrick. He had just emerged from the door at the top of the outside flight of stairs.

"I've got help," she said, introducing her secretary's brother to Michael, Patrick, and Anthony.

After introductions were done and it was clear that Lily didn't have enough furniture to keep even one person very busy, the Frascato brothers headed back upstairs. "Well, if you need any help, don't hesitate to call. We'll be working up here all day," said Patrick.

She nodded and thanked him.

"So what about the dog?" asked Michael.

"I get him tomorrow," she said. Lily had spoken to Don Jones the day after she'd seen the apartment. He'd explained that no one else in the office had even asked about Sam. He was hers if she wanted him and she did. Don was going to bring him over first thing the next morning.

Chapter Six

After the van left and Michael and his brothers went back to work upstairs, Lily began to settle into her new apartment. Before she started to unpack she set up her CD player and put some of her favorites into the machine, including Bruce Springsteen, Jamie Cullum, and Counting Crows and turned the volume up loud. Smiling to herself over the fact that she could listen to whatever music she wanted, she began to unpack. This was the first time she'd really been on her own and she was going to like it.

She quickly hung up her clothes and made up her bed with new sheets she'd picked up the day before, covering them with the quilt her grandmother had made her on the occasion of her setting off for law school. She smoothed it out over the pillows as she thought about the woman who had been her champion and in-spiration growing up. Her grandmother had become a widow at thirty and had raised her mother alone. But instead of being harsh and demanding, as sometimes Lily's mother was, Grandma had been Lily's ally all through her growing up years. She was the one Lily turned to when she felt no one understood her or when she doubted her mother's love for her. Grandma's love was constant and her support consistent. When Grandma had passed away the year before, Lily felt the loss enormously and knew that from then on she would have to be her own champion. She'd managed fine, Grandma had done her job well, but at times like this Lily wished she could pick up the phone and tell Grandma all about the new apartment and maybe even about Michael and his brothers and how good they'd been to her.

After the bed was made, she went into the living room and considered what to do next. There wasn't much time before Arlene, her new boyfriend, and the boyfriend's frat brother would be showing up. It was five and they were coming by at seven o'clock to pick her up. Although Arlene had suggested eating in Lily's new neighborhood, Lily had no idea where to go. Of course she could have asked Michael and his brothers for a recommendation, but she wasn't sure how much she wanted them to be involved in her social life, particularly since she didn't even know Arlene's boyfriend or his friend. From past experience she knew Arlene's taste in men could sometimes be questionable.

She also suspected that the three brothers would be happy to get involved in her personal life and give her all kinds of advice. They'd already told her where to buy her groceries and which dry cleaner was the best. She was grateful for the information, but not sure how much more involvement she wanted. Although she had never lived alone before, she'd been on her own for so long that it felt weird to have people watching out for her. Lily's own brothers had never paid her much mind. They were five and seven years older than she and had been out of the house by the time she got to high school. She saw them on the holidays and they called one another on their birthdays. Other than that they didn't have much to do with one another. Lily's dad had always put work first so she never had much to do with him when she was growing up. Now when she did go home, she found that they didn't have a lot to say to each other. On the other hand, Lily's mother would have loved to be more involved in Lily's life, but Lily really didn't welcome that intrusion. Ever since Lily hit adolescence and started to have a mind of her own, she and her mother rarely saw eye to eye. Most recently Lily's decision to go to law school and then practice in the inner cities of New Jersey were both obvious disappointments to her mother. Lately, the only thing she and her mother agreed on was Lily's relationship with Josh. Lily's mom loved Josh and thought he was the perfect boyfriend. Her only complaint was that Lily did not yet have a diamond, though she seemed to be placated by the fact that right now Josh was paving the way for greatness by serving the less fortunate. Lily sometimes wondered if her mother's fondness for Josh had more to do with the fact that he was a doctor and would someday make good money than with his personality. But at least they agreed about Josh and when Lily did speak to her mother she could steer the conversation in that direction whenever her mother became critical of the rest of her life. So Lily was wary of anyone trying to look too closely at what she was up to. In her experience it usually was an unfortunate intrusion.

She was almost relieved when Michael stopped by at five thirty to let her know they were quitting for the day. "We probably won't be around tomorrow so if you need anything moved, let me know now," he said.

"I'm fine," she said. "I really don't have very much stuff so it doesn't matter where it is." That was the truth. Besides the few pieces of furniture, she had a set of dishes and three wineglasses that her mother had given her, and a sterling silver set for twelve that had been left to her by her grandmother. She also had a TV, DVD player, and an iPod docking station, but she didn't have a couch or even a chair for the living room. Her plan was to check on Craigslist, figuring she'd be able to pick up some furniture that way. She also intended to make a trip to one of the nearby discount stores to buy some glasses and coffee mugs, and maybe even a few throw rugs. If she added plants and fresh flowers, the place would be fine. Come the spring, she would deal with the garden. She already was planning what she was going to grow and figured she would buy some tulip bulbs sometime in the next few weeks. Six months from now, when she had recovered from this spending spree, she would be able to buy some furniture for the patio.

But now she didn't even have anywhere for anyone

to sit except in the kitchen and Arlene and these two guys would be over in an hour. She finished setting up the television and DVD player on the floor, put her plants on a mat by the sliding door, and stacked the four plates and three glasses in the cabinet. When that was done, she grabbed her coat and pocketbook and took off down the street. She'd noticed a liquor store and a small grocery around the corner. Hopefully she'd be able to find a decent bottle of wine, a few bottles of beer, and some cheese and crackers. They might even sell glasses. If they didn't she supposed she could drink her wine in a coffee mug.

The phone was ringing when she got back from the store. It was Josh returning her call. She'd called him earlier with her new number since she already had her phone hooked up, thanks to Michael's brothers. As she put the wine in the freezer to chill and rinsed out the newly purchased glasses, she filled him in on the day's events and the fact that she was going out that night with Arlene. She told him about Arlene's new boyfriend and the friend he was bringing.

"It shouldn't be a late night," said Lily, hoping she didn't sound as defensive as she felt. Josh had always encouraged her to go out, saying that at their age they shouldn't be sitting at home all the time just because they were so far apart. She'd taken him at his word, but sometimes, like tonight, she wasn't sure if he really meant it. It was his job that kept them apart, but for some reason she always felt guilty when she went out and had fun.

"I've decided to get a dog," she told him, glad for some news that didn't involve either of them or their social lives.

"Are you serious?"

"Yes," she said, wondering why she was becoming irritated. Of course she was serious. What was wrong with getting a dog?

Josh continued. "I can't believe you did that. Who's going to take care of the dog when you're at work?"

"His former owner says he'll be fine."

"Of course he said that. He wanted to get rid of it. But what are you going to do?"

"I'm sure I'll manage," Lily answered, trying to keep the frost from her voice.

"What about when you come out to see me?"

"How often do I do that?" she said. "When I do I can leave him at a kennel. He'll be good company and good for protection."

"That's true," said Josh. "Is the neighborhood dangerous?"

"Of course not. What are you up to?" she asked, desperate to get off the subject of the dog.

"Just going to get a pizza and maybe a video," he said. "Today was intense and tomorrow doesn't look any better."

She shouldn't have been surprised. He hardly ever went out, always working or recovering. She guessed she should be happy she didn't have to wonder where he was or worry that he wasn't being faithful.

When she hung up she was feeling irritated and frustrated by their conversation. It was not the first time she wished they weren't so far apart. But now was not the time to think about it. It was six thirty and she still had to shower.

By the time the doorbell rang, promptly at seven, she had changed into her good jeans and a skinny sweater. She brushed back her hair from her face and checked her makeup to be sure she didn't have any smudges, and went to answer the door.

Arlene introduced her boyfriend, Fred, a tall, lanky, nondescript guy, and his frat brother Al. Al was about Lily's height, five feet seven, small-boned and so compact that Lily wondered if she outweighed him. If she didn't, it was only because she hadn't had a chance to eat all day. In any case, she was glad that she was not wearing heels. Even if he really wasn't her date, she didn't want to tower over him.

"The apartment is great," said Arlene, looking into the living room from the entranceway. "You're going to give us a tour?"

"Sure," said Lily, "though there isn't too much to see."

She'd taken their coats, and hung them in the otherwise empty closet after being introduced to the two men. As she led the way into the living room, she turned on the outside light so they could see the patio. Arlene explained that Al, like Fred, worked with computers. "Something to do with mainframes and networking," said Arlene, "so they're no good with fixing our computers."

"Was that your major in college?" Lily asked Al, hoping they would have something to say to each other. What she knew about computers could fit into a teacup.

Al shook his head. "Nope. I majored in business, with a minor in accounting."

Lily nodded. She knew even less about accounting.

She showed her guests the rest of the apartment, glad that Arlene had gotten to see it right away. Arlene was appropriately enthused and gave her some ideas on where to place her bed, where to find cheap bookcases, since Lily's books were stacked knee-deep in her bedroom against one wall, and what color she might paint the bathroom if Michael and his brothers didn't mind.

The tour done, Lily led them back to the kitchen where she'd set out the cheese and crackers. "How about a glass of wine or a beer before we head out," she said.

Both men took the offered beer and Lily poured a glass of wine for herself and Arlene.

After taking a long sip, Fred shook his head and looked at her questioningly. "Why Jersey City?" he said.

Lily looked at him for a minute to see if he was going to elaborate on his question. When he didn't say anything more, she tried to make sense of it. "You mean as opposed to . . ." She waited, hoping he would fill in the blank. He didn't. She looked to the others to see if they too had this question and when they looked at her blankly, she continued. "Why Jersey City instead of Hoboken? Because I can't afford to live by myself in Hoboken, same with the City."

"But Jersey City? Aren't you afraid of walking down here by yourself? Wouldn't you rather be out in a pretty suburb in a complex with a pool and tennis courts?"

"Oh, I see what you mean," said Lily, but not sure how to answer him. He sounded too much like her mother.

Arlene came to the rescue. "Lily likes the city," she said. She turned to Lily. "Fred doesn't understand why anyone would want to live in a city when there are so many new and clean garden apartments out in Morris County."

Just like her mother.

"Even in Essex County," said Fred. "Places like Cedar Grove have apartments."

Lily shrugged and tried to smile. "What about you, Al?" she said. "You live in the suburbs?"

Al nodded. "Yup," he said. "A place just like Fred's with a swimming pool and tennis courts. Only difference is that it's on the west coast, in Seattle."

"I see," said Lily. It was going to be a long night. If she wasn't afraid of offending Arlene she would have feigned a headache and sent them on their way.

It didn't get any better after that. When they got to the restaurant, a steakhouse in Hoboken that she and Jessica had picked because you didn't need a reservation, it was crowded, so they had to wait at the bar. While they stood cheek to jowl with the other patrons, holding on to their drinks, Fred told them all about how well he was doing and Al chimed in that he also was doing well. Each man had a work story involving mainframes and Internet access. They seemed contented to talk to each other and didn't seem to notice that neither Lily nor Arlene participated. Lily didn't know enough to contribute to the computer conversation and she couldn't figure out how to gracefully change the subject.

It was the same during dinner so Lily tried to talk to Arlene, but each time she started to speak one of the men would look her way and scowl. She even tried to think of a war story from her job, but realized that this was not a crowd that would think anything to do with child abuse was fit conversation for a social evening. Lily did notice that Arlene seemed to find Fred interesting and that she didn't seem to feel the need to contribute with her share of work war stories. Fortunately the evening ended early. Al had a plane to catch first thing in the morning and Fred said he had to get to the office to work on an emergency. They dropped Lily off at ten. When Al walked her to her door to make sure that she was safely home he told her he'd had a great evening. Lily was speechless and glad she had Josh. Arlene often warned her that she should count her lucky stars that she had Josh. After tonight, Lily could see what Arlene meant.

Sam, the dog, was delivered to her bright and early the next morning. Don was at the door shortly before nine. "Hope you don't mind," he said, "but we're going to be gone all day so it seemed best to bring him over to you first thing."

"I don't," she said, "but aren't you going to give me instructions?"

"Have you ever had a dog?" he asked.

She nodded. She had one as a kid, though they hadn't had the dog for long. Her father had turned out to be allergic to him. But she didn't tell that to Don for fear he might think she wasn't qualified to take Sam.

"Well then you know. Feed him twice a day. Walk him more than that, and pick up after him." He placed a bag of dog food on the table and the leash beside it. Sam was running around in circles sniffing at everything and wagging his tail.

"What about during the day?" she asked. "Did you leave him alone?" Maybe Josh had a point. What if the dog needed constant attention?

Don looked surprised at her question. "My wife took care of him during the day."

"And before that?"

"I had a roommate."

"But I don't." She didn't want Josh to be right.

Don shrugged. "He should be okay. Take him for a long run in the morning and then see what happens." He looked at his watch. "Hate to do this to you but I really got to run. My wife is waiting for me at home. We're going to see her family in New York."

Lily nodded and motioned for him to go. "We'll be fine." She looked at the dog. "Right, Sam?" Sam looked back at her questioningly. He didn't seem so certain that Lily had it all in hand. Maybe he understood the conversation about what to do during the day and was thinking he wasn't going to like it here. In any case, he started to whine as Don headed to the door. When Don closed the door behind him, Sam turned and looked at Lily and then began to howl.

Fortunately there were no other tenants in the building, but Lily figured the only solution to whatever was ailing Sam was a good long walk. Once outside, she realized it gave her a chance to see the neighborhood. It was still early enough that the streets were nearly empty. Lily walked along with Sam and studied the brownstones lining the four streets that made up the square surrounding Hamilton Park. Many of them looked as if they'd been renovated, though it was impossible to tell if they were divided into apartments or continued to be single-family homes. Lily smiled to herself. It was a pretty neighborhood and she thought she was going to like living there. Suddenly Sam started to drag her across the street in the direction of the park to where there was a couple walking a retriever that looked a lot like Sam. She didn't know if Sam was friendly or not, but now would be the time to find out. As the two dogs circled each other and tangled up their owners, Lily greeted the couple that owned the other dog. Lily started to apologize, but the woman interrupted her.

"No need," she said. "They're all like that, especially when they're puppies. How old is your dog?"

Lily shook her head. "Four years old, I think. I just got him this morning."

The woman looked bemused. "Really! Where from?"

Lily explained about Don and his situation on the home front.

The woman nodded sympathetically. "Well, at least you'll be able to find out his history easily enough. It's good to know." She paused as she focused on pulling her dog away from a clump of flowers that it was about to eat. "You also should make sure his shots are up-to-date."

Lily nodded. "I think they are, but Don was in such a rush he hardly told me much of anything. I'll find out about it all tomorrow," she said quickly. She didn't want the woman reporting her to the ASPCA for medical neglect.

Lily wondered what else she didn't know as she continued on her walk. Sam certainly seemed to like being outside, but what about inside? Did he chew things? And how did he like being left alone? Only time would tell—and Michael and his brothers, if they were there during the day working on the house.

Dealing with Sam was easier than she imagined. Taking Don's advice, she'd gone for a run with him first thing the following morning. Still hesitant about leaving him alone for the whole day, she'd run into Patrick when she was coming back from her first morning run. After Sam and Patrick introduced themselves and became instant friends, Patrick asked her what she intended to do about the dog during the day.

Lily shrugged. "I was hoping he could last until I got home at night."

"What time do you get home?"

Lily shrugged again. "It really does vary, depending what's going on at work. I was hoping to get back by six."

"Do you want one of us to take him out in the middle of the day?" he asked.

"You'd do that for me?"

He smiled and nodded. "Sure. We're here every day, at least for the time being while we fix up this building. Even when it's done we'll be in the neighborhood." He paused and sighed. "At least that's the plan. Anyway, as long as we're working around here, one of us can take him out. We can even pick him up and bring him along when we go down to the deli to pick up sandwiches at lunchtime." He looked down at the dog. "If he plays his cards right and behaves himself, we might even let him hang out with us all day."

It was too good to be true. "What can I do to repay you?"

Patrick shook his head. "Don't be silly. I'm sure you'll return the favor one way or another now that you're living here. And I'm glad to do it. Sam seems like a great dog."

She nodded. That was true. So far Sam had proven to be very good company. After their walk on Sunday he'd stuck by her while she continued to settle into the apartment. When she was stowing away her clothes in her bedroom and arranging her books in the bookcases on either side of the fireplace in the living room, he lay on the floor close by. When she made soup, he sat on the kitchen floor and watched her every move. Finally, at the end of the day when she made a fire and fashioned a makeshift bed out of pillows in front of it and settled down to read, Sam curled up beside her. Lily was beginning to understand why people put up with the responsibility of a dog. They did appear to be worth the effort. She couldn't wait to tell Josh.

Chapter Seven

Although Lily saw Anthony and Patrick almost every day, she did not see Michael until court later the following week. Even then she didn't have a chance to talk to him about the apartment or the fact that his brothers were taking care of Sam, although she suspected he already knew. The three brothers were obviously very close. When she did talk to Michael it was about one of her cases. The first matter heard that morning involved Ms. Smith, a single mother with three small children. She had originally become involved with the social service agency because she had been evicted from her apartment for not paying the rent. Although she had a job as a waitress, she could not find another apartment that she could afford. She spent one night staying with friends, but on the second night one of the men living in the apartment had demanded that she sleep with him in exchange for staying there. She immediately left the apartment with her three kids. That had been last January when the temperature was below freezing. Instead of going to a shelter, which she said was dangerous, she had gone to a local hospital hoping they would let her and her kids stay there. The hospital called the DYFS. When it became clear that she had no place to live except for the shelter, which she refused to stay in, she signed an agreement to put her children in foster care until she could find a home. Three months ago she had found an apartment and the children were returned to her. But when the caseworker went out to the apartment just to make sure everything was okay, she and the children were gone. The landlord had explained that she'd been evicted because she hadn't paid her rent.

The case was scheduled for that morning and the agency wanted Lily to ask that the children be removed from their mother if she showed up for court. If Ms. Smith did not appear, Lily was supposed to ask for a bench warrant so Ms. Smith could be arrested and brought in for questioning. Everyone was concerned that Ms. Smith was living in the park, or worse. Lily had spent the past weeks wondering and worrying about where Ms. Smith and the kids were and if they were okay. The case was called and Ms. Smith was not there. When Lily explained the situation, the judge agreed to issue the warrant.

About an hour later, between cases when the judge took a brief recess and got off the bench, Michael came up behind Lily. "Can I speak to you for a minute?"

"Sure." She was puzzled. It was unusual for him to talk to her when court was in session.

"Ms. Smith just got here," he said.

Lily was surprised she'd shown up. "Are her kids with her?"

He nodded.

"You tell her we already heard the case?"

He nodded again. "I think you should come out and see her," he added, "when you get a chance."

She looked at him in surprise. She usually did not go out and see the families. That was the caseworker's job, and because it might appear to be infringing on the caseworker's territory to get personally involved with the defendants Lily always avoided the contact.

"I think you might change your mind about removing the kids," said Michael.

She gave him a sharp look. This was the first time since she'd been in Paterson that Michael had expressed an opinion on what the social service agency did about the children and their parents.

"Come out at the next break, before you do anything. Okay?" he said as the judge came back into the courtroom.

She nodded.

When she went out in the hall she found Ms. Smith sitting on one of the benches flanked by her three children. The two young boys sat on one side and her daughter on the other. The little girl, who at six was the oldest of the three, looked up when Lily approached, and responded to Lily with a smile. Then she tugged at her mother's arm and pointed in Lily's direction.

Lily returned the child's smile and then turned to her mother. "Ms. Smith," said Lily, "you may remember from the last hearing that I'm the lawyer for the children's service agency. We're happy to see you here today. We've been concerned about your whereabouts."

The women nodded, looking apprehensive. Before she had a chance to say anything, the little girl looked up at Lily. "We had to come with Mama today because there isn't any school." She continued, "I'm Julia and this is my mommy," she said. "These are my brothers, Will and Chris," she added pointing to them.

The mother sighed. "It's true. Today is a school holiday so I had to bring them."

The little girl reached up and pulled Lily's hand. Lily looked over at her. "This," she said, indicating the pink jacket that she was wearing, "is my new jacket. Mommy got it for me and these," she said, extending her feet, "are my new shoes."

Lily looked down at her and smiled, mindful of the fact that as the state lawyer she must not become personally involved with the families that her client assisted. However, a six-year-old would not understand if Lily ignored her. "Very nice," she said, crouching down so she was eye level with the child. "Do your brothers have new shoes too?"

One of the boys, who Lily remembered was four, suddenly swung his legs up, pointed to his feet, and nodded. "New shoes," he said quietly with evident pride.

Lily felt a tap on her shoulder and she stood up to face Michael, who motioned for her to follow him down the hall, presumably out of earshot of the woman and her kids.

"See what I mean?" he said softly. "Don't you think you should give her another chance?"

Lily shook her head. "It's not my call." She paused. "She needs to give the agency a reasonable explanation of where's she's been so they know she's safe, and with her history she is going to have to cooperate and show them. It's not a decision I can make on my own."

It might not be her call, but from what she could see, Michael was right. The children were obviously well taken care of and attached to one another. In her experience, if they took the children into custody they would probably end up in three different foster homes. That was not a solution that really worked for anybody. On the other hand, was Ms. Smith's living arrangement stable? This family couldn't keep moving from place to place.

Lily called the caseworker over and asked her to speak with Ms. Smith. Ten minutes later the worker returned to Lily.

"If what Ms. Smith is telling me is true, than Michael is right. We shouldn't remove these kids."

"What was her explanation?" asked Lily.

"She says that after she got evicted from her apartment she went to her mother's. She says she's been staying there with her mother and her mother's boyfriend. They had an extra room and were happy to have Ms. Smith help out with the groceries. As you know, Ms. Smith has a job as a waitress, so it's not as if she doesn't work. It's just that the money doesn't go very far with rent and feeding herself and the three kids. Anyway, everything was fine there until a few nights ago when her mother got drunk and got into a fight with her boyfriend. Ms. Smith tried to stop the fight so her mother got mad at her instead and blamed Ms. Smith for the fact that her boyfriend walked out on her. After that she threw Ms. Smith and the kids out. Ms. Smith's been looking for a place to live ever since." The worker looked at Lily. "And you know how hard it is to find housing around here. There's just not enough to go around."

Lily nodded. "So where's she been staying?"

"She broke down and went to a shelter here in Paterson, but she thinks she has a line up on a place. That's what I've got to check out."

"And why was she late today?"

"It's three buses from the shelter to here. She missed one of the connections and had to wait." The worker shook her head. "It couldn't have been easy dragging the three kids across town like that."

"So you think we should consider letting her keep the kids?"

The worker nodded. "Of course, I'll have to check out what she's told me and look at the home, but assuming it's all true, I think the kids would be better off with her than in foster care." The worker shrugged. "She still needs to learn to keep in touch with me, but I can't really blame her. She doesn't have a cell phone and it's not always easy to find a phone."

Lily nodded. There was no telling what a child might get in foster care. Sometimes it was terrific, but there were other times, much publicized, where the kids where in as much danger as they would be with their own parents.

Lily called the office and told them what was happening, including the caseworker's observations. After some convincing, including a chat with the worker's supervisor, they agreed to the plan of assessing the apartment Ms. Smith had found, as well as checking out her story, before asking to have the kids taken from her. The next step was to ask the court to go along with the new plan. She'd also have to get Maria, as the children's lawyer, to agree to it too.

She went back inside the courtroom and approached the bench. The judge wasn't out yet, but his clerk was. "Tracy?" she said. "We're going to be asking for the Smith case to be heard again."

Tracy sighed heavily and flipped back her hair. "You better have a good excuse. We've got a big calendar and you know the judge wants to finish early today."

Lily counted to ten. Tracy was tougher than the judge would ever be, but she was the gatekeeper and if Lily couldn't get by her she wouldn't even have a chance to ask the judge to reconsider his decision to remove the kids. "Tracy," she said using her most persuasive voice, all the while hoping she didn't sound like she was groveling. "We've got particular circumstances. Ms. Smith has just shown up and has an explanation."

"Better be a good one. You know the judge hates it when people are late for court."

Lily nodded, gritted her teeth, and smiled. "I do know that, but why don't we let the judge decide if the explanation is a good one?"

Tracy's eyes narrowed and Lily could have bit her

tongue. She had to remember that Tracy didn't like her authority questioned.

"Tracy," said Michael, who must have just come into the courtroom and overheard their conversation. "Give the lady a break! She was late because she was getting her kids ready to come here. Wait until you've got three rug rats to get dressed in the morning and see if you're on time for work."

"Don't hassle me, Michael. You know I don't like it when you side with them!" Sighing heavily, she turned to Lily and shrugged. "All right, all right, I can see I'm being outnumbered. I'll let the judge know you want to put Smith back on the calendar. Anything else, or can we move on?"

Lily shook her head. "That's it, and in fact, the rest of the calendar looks pretty quick."

Maria agreed with Lily's proposal and the judge was easy to convince; in fact, much easier than anyone. At the end of the day, after all their cases were heard, Lily asked to approach the bench and speak to the judge off the record. "Your Honor," she said, "I want to thank you for reconsidering your decision on the Smith case."

Judge Keegan peered down at her, looking slightly puzzled. "I was glad to keep them with their mother. I really don't like to remove kids. The longer I do this work the more I think we do more harm than good when we remove them, especially when they're going to foster homes instead of relatives. I was glad you gave me a reason."

"It was Michael," she said. "He's the one who made

me go out in the hall and meet Ms. Smith and her children."

"Interesting," said Judge Keegan, looking thoughtful. "I always thought Michael had good instincts, but I hadn't realized he was starting to participate in the cases. Michael," said Judge Keegan, "something special about the Smiths?"

Michael approached from the back of the courtroom. He shook his head. "Not really. It was just obvious that they were good kids. Didn't think they got that way all by themselves. Their mother had to do something right."

The judge shrugged. "But it's not the first time we've had kids we didn't want to see in foster care."

Michael nodded and then smiled. "Maybe it's just the first time I feel like we have a state attorney who will listen."

The judge arched his eyebrows speculatively, but didn't say anything. Lily merely lowered her head and pretended to be focused on the documents stacked at the table. The judge cleared his throat. "Well, if that's all we've got for today, I'm going to head out. The wife has plans for me."

Because court ended at four, it was too late to go back to the office, so Lily got home a bit earlier than usual. The dog wasn't in the apartment so she went upstairs to the apartment Michael's brothers were working on to see if Sam was there. When she found the door to the apartment ajar, she walked in, calling out Patrick and Anthony's names. Patrick responded and, following his voice, she found them all in the far end of the apartment. Sam was curled up in the middle of the construction site looking quite content, though he did acknowledge her presence with a thump of his tail.

"I hope he hasn't been a nuisance," she said.

"He's been a good boy," said Patrick. "Right, Sam?"

Sam thumped his tail again.

"Has he been here all day?" asked Lily.

Patrick shook his head. "Only since lunchtime. We took him out when we went and got the sandwiches and then when he was so easy we figured he might as well hang out with us for the rest of the day. He's obviously very social and we figured he gets lonely down there."

Lily looked over at Anthony, who nodded in agreement. As Patrick talked, she looked around the room that they were working on. It was the living room and mirrored hers, except instead of sliding doors out to the garden it had a small balcony overlooking the yard.

"Is this apartment the same size as mine?" she asked.

"Bigger," said Patrick "The first floor is just about the same but this one is a duplex so there's a whole other level. Want a tour?"

"Sure," she said.

Both brothers stopped what they were doing and stood up. "This room is almost done," said Anthony. "Tomorrow we're going to paint it. Over here," he said, pointing to the doorway off the living room, "is the kitchen. We'll do that last. Come on over to the other side," he said, walking over to the other end of the living room where there was another opening. This is one bedroom," he said, pointing in to a room not unlike Lily's. "Upstairs are two more and a bath. The bath down here is the same size as yours. But we haven't done anything on it yet."

Lily followed them from room to room taking it all in.

"What do you think?" asked the two brothers, almost in unison.

"Great," said Lily. "You do nice work."

"Our biggest problem is picking out the tiles and fixtures for the bathroom and the kitchen. To be honest we don't have a clue."

"What do you mean? You did a nice job downstairs."

Anthony shook his head. "We didn't pick those out. My ex-girlfriend did."

Anthony and Patrick suddenly looked at each other and then at Lily. "What about you? Can you do that?"

"What do you mean?" she asked.

"Are you any good at picking out stuff?"

She shrugged. "I don't know. I guess I can. I mean, I'm not afraid to. I know what I like."

"Great!" said Anthony rubbing his hands together. "Come with me."

He led her into the kitchen that was still a large empty space. "As you can see we haven't even picked the appliances."

Lily must have looked worried.

"Don't worry," he said. "We know where we're going to put them and we've got the catalogues. We just couldn't decide. Can you do that for us?"

She shrugged. "Sure." It sounded like fun.

"You're a lifesaver," said Patrick. "We're running out of time and didn't know where to turn."

"What do you mean?"

"We should have a tenant in here by next month if we're going to keep to budget so we need to get stuff ordered right away."

An hour later Lily had picked out the tile for the two bathrooms: white with cobalt blue trim. For the kitchen floor she chose sand-colored Spanish tile and for the countertops, granite in shades of tan, brown, and coral to match the floor. She was starting in on the appliances, leaning toward the same ones that were in her apartment, when Michael walked into the kitchen. He looked from his brothers, who were sitting on the floor with the dog, to Lily who was sitting cross-legged beside them poring over catalogues. "Okay, I give up. What's going on?"

"Hey, Michael, I think we've got our solution!" said Patrick, waving the samples Lily had picked out.

"This girl's got an eye," said Anthony.

"I just stopped by—" began Lily.

Michael again looked from one to the other before stopping and staring at Lily. "Can someone please explain?"

She smiled weakly. "They asked me to pick out tiles and stuff."

"And you can?" he asked.

She nodded. "I think so. I don't understand what's so hard about it. But I don't want to intrude—"

He shook his head. "Believe me, you are not intruding. We are happy for any help we can get." He paused for a minute as if thinking and then turned back to Lily. "Do you want to go look at the building we just bought?"

"What? Now?"

Michael started to nod, but after looking at his watch, shook his head with a sigh. "I guess it's getting late and I've got practice. But it doesn't have to be tonight. What about another time? Would you be interested?"

"Sure," she said. "Actually, I'd love to. I really like these old buildings."

"Really?" he said. "That's great. What's a good day for you? Would Sunday work? We could also look at a building we're thinking of buying."

"Sure," she said. It sounded like fun; certainly tonight had been. "But you don't really need my input. You obviously know what you're doing. This place is proof."

Michael shook his head. "You don't understand. The three of us can build anything. We know the neighborhoods and we know construction. We even can do electrical and plumbing, painting and wallpaper. But none of us are strong on decorating and that sort of thing. If you don't mind . . ." He paused and looked at his brothers who nodded in agreement. "We really could use the help."

She believed him. They really did act like they wanted her opinion. She smiled. "I'll be glad to," she said and then motioned toward Sam. "Besides, you're looking after my dog." She got up and looked at the dog. "Want to go for a walk?" she asked. She wasn't sure if he'd want to leave his new friends. However, he wagged his tail and ran straight for the door. He was still hers. She turned to Anthony to ask about the leash when her cell phone rang. She rummaged in her purse as it insistently rang and she finally retrieved it on the fourth ring. It was Josh. Her heart sank. Right now he was just about the last person that she wanted to hear from. Of course she loved him and she wasn't trying to keep her relationship with him a secret, but conversations with Josh were never short or playful. She couldn't imagine having one in their presence.

"Excuse me," she said, looking up at the three men who were all watching her with more than casual interest. She spoke into the phone. "Let me call you back. I'm in the middle of something." She paused and listened to Josh's predictable objections. "It's a crisis. I'll call you as soon as I can." She disconnected and looked up, dreading to see their reaction.

None of them were looking at her. Michael had walked to the other side of the room and appeared to be carefully examining the paint job. Anthony had retrieved the leash and was focused on putting it on Sam. Patrick had ducked down behind the counter and seemed to be checking the plumbing.

"Got to go," she said brightly. "Thanks again for looking after Sam."

Michael walked her to the door. "Sunday about two?" he asked. "I really want to hear what you think about those buildings. Pat and Anthony think you're Jersey City's answer to Martha Stewart."

She looked up at him and grinned, surprised at how much it pleased her that Michael and his brothers thought she was talented. "Not quite. Besides the fact that I haven't been to jail," she said, "there's a big difference between picking out some tiles and being an interior designer. I'm just not intimidated by color."

Michael shrugged. "Well, whatever, it's obvious that
you have a lot of style," he said, pointing to what she was
wearing, a designer suit she found on one of her forays at
the outlets. "And you were a big help. We appreciate it."
   As he opened the door, she looked up at him. "Thanks
for what you did today," she said.
   "What do you mean?" he asked.
   "You know you didn't have to put yourself out like
that for Ms. Smith. By speaking out like that you saved
those kids from foster care."
   He shook his head. "You wouldn't have let them go."
   "I might have," she said. "I had instructions from my
client. You're the one who observed the mother and
thought she deserved a break. I wouldn't have known
about her if you hadn't brought it to my attention."
   He looked pleased but slightly embarrassed. "I was
glad to do it. They seemed like good kids."
   She grinned. "I agree. And it makes me feel better
that they are with their mother tonight instead of being
in a strange foster home."
   When he nodded in agreement, their eyes met and
Lily felt a sudden strong connection that reached down
into her stomach. Quickly, she turned away and headed
down the stairs. She needed to give Sam a walk and call
Josh back and not think about what just happened. It
didn't make any sense.

   Lily called Josh as soon as she got back from walking Sam and explained what had been happening when
he called earlier.
   "They are asking you for advice about the color of

what they're installing in the kitchen?" he said, sounding more than dubious.

"Yes," she said, hating the fact that she sounded defensive. "They think I'm really talented. That I've got a good eye for color." She didn't bother with the Martha Stewart comment. She could only imagine what Josh's response to that would be.

"I guess it's nice that you're making friends," he said, "and that they're looking out for your dog. You're lucky. That dog could be a real albatross. I don't know what you were thinking when you got him."

She sighed. Josh could be so practical and although he might have a point—what would she have done if Michael's brothers hadn't been around to take Sam out during the day—she wished he would leave it alone.

"How was your day?" she asked. "Any interesting cases?"

"Not really," he said. "Same old, same old. Unfortunately, with poverty, it all starts to look the same."

Thinking about her day and Ms. Smith's dilemma, she agreed. Unfortunately, that was true in her business as well. There was no way that lady would be in the family court if she could afford an apartment on her own.

Chapter Eight

On Friday when Lily got to the office her message light was on. One of the caseworkers in the Paterson office had left a message asking her to call back as soon as she got in.

"We need you to go to court for us today," said Irene, the caseworker in charge of litigation, when Lily returned the call.

It had to be an emergency. No one wanted to be in court on a Friday afternoon. It meant the judge would be looking at his watch wondering if she and the agency were going to delay the start of his weekend.

"Tell me what's going on," said Lily. Irene was a veteran so she knew it had to be an emergency.

"We've got an abandoned baby."

"Give me the specifics," said Lily. If the baby was legally abandoned the case would be very straightforward. To prevent babies from being left in Dumpsters to die, New Jersey had passed a law that allowed a parent to drop a baby off at a hospital, police station, or firehouse with no questions asked and no penalty. That rarely happened. But no matter how a baby was abandoned, Lily would have to file. There had to be someone legally responsible for the child. She just needed to know the facts to make sure it would pass legal muster and satisfy Judge Keegan.

"This child is three days old," said Irene. "His mother came into the hospital, gave birth, and then left."

"Did she name the baby before she disappeared?" That would be a good indication of how involved the mother was. No name usually showed a complete lack of interest.

"Nope."

"Do we have the mother's identity or her address or any information on the father?"

"Zilch. The mother gave a fake name and a phony address. No father identified. Baby is suffering drug withdrawal so the mother was obviously an addict. Probably left to get her fix," Irene added.

"Other than the withdrawal, how is the baby doing?" asked Lily.

"Surprisingly well. And he is a good size," said Irene. "Over seven pounds."

That was good. His healthy size would improve his chances to develop normally. "So what is your plan for him?" asked Lily.

"It's a perfect scenario for a quick adoption. We've already found him a home—a couple who have been waiting for a baby to adopt—so we just need to get custody so we can authorize any medical tests and be able to give him to the couple when he's medically cleared and ready for discharge."

"Sounds like a plan," said Lily. "When can you have the complaint ready for me to review and sign?" she asked.

"I should have it by one o'clock," said Irene.

That meant two o'clock since Irene operated in her own time zone. Lily calculated that if she went over to the Paterson office at two, reviewed and signed the complaint when she got there, they could be in court by three. She just needed to call the court and Maria to alert them about what was going on. The judge was not the only one who liked to slip out before five on Fridays, so she needed to give everyone a heads-up.

She packed up her cases, put on her coat, and was walking down the hall headed for the door when a voice called out.

"Hey, Lily, where are you off to?"

She turned to see Don Jones in the doorway of his office.

"How's Sam?" he asked. "Working out all right?"

She nodded. "He's a great dog."

He nodded dolefully. "Sure is. I hated to give him up. It was almost a deal breaker."

"Excuse me?"

He grinned sheepishly. "Just kidding. I wouldn't leave my wife over a dog." He shook his head. "But it wasn't easy letting him go. I'm happy to hear he's working out all right." He cocked his head and looked over at Lily. "I take it there've been no problems."

"Absolutely none. He's great. If you want, come by and see him," she said.

He shook his head. "I'd just feel bad. But I'm glad he's got a good home."

Lily drove from her office in Newark to the local social service agency office in Paterson, reviewed and signed the complaint and then headed over to court. When she walked into the courtroom, the judge wasn't on the bench yet, but Michael was up in the front of the courtroom talking to Tracy who, as usual, was playing some game on her computer.

"We're still looking at bands," she said. "Tonight we have to go up to a club in Clifton and tomorrow we're going to stop by a reception in Wayne." She shook her head. "It's not easy planning something like this. I don't think I'm going to get it all done in the year that I've got.

"So what about you?" she continued. "You haven't been sharing any war stories. Still seeing that girl from Bayonne?"

Lily realized that she was waiting for the answer. Mortified at the idea that she might be inadvertently eavesdropping, she started moving the chairs at the counsel's table so they would know someone was there. They both turned to look at her just as Maria arrived breathless and harried.

"Can't believe you wait until Friday afternoon to file a complaint," said Tracy looking up from her computer game and over at Lily.

Lily shook her head. Tracy was such a pain, but she

had to be dealt with. "Sometimes it's necessary. Poor baby needs to have someone responsible for him."

Suddenly, the judge came in so she was saved from further conversation with Tracy. Quickly and succinctly, Lily put the relevant information about the abandoned baby on the record; Maria agreed with the agency's assessment and the judge, just as quickly, determined that there was sufficient reason for the state to obtain custody. He nodded to Lily and Maria and left the bench. He would go back to his chambers and wait, impatiently, Lily was sure, for her to fill in the necessary language required by federal regulations so he could sign the complaint and be done for the day.

Tracy, who had continued to play solitaire during the brief hearing, looked up from her computer. "So who's going to name the baby?"

Lily shook her head instead of answering, knowing what was coming next.

"I don't see why you won't let me name him," said Tracy.

"She already explained to you that the world doesn't need another Christopher," said Michael, who was standing nearby.

Tracy tossed her head and frowned. "I happen to think Christopher is a beautiful name."

Lily looked up from filling out the forms. "It is a beautiful name. It's just not our place to name this baby." She finished reviewing the document and got up. "Besides, Michael's right. We can't name every abandoned baby that comes through this courtroom Christopher."

"Only the boys," said Tracy. "I like Madison if it's a girl."

Maria shook her head and Michael rolled his eyes. Tracy pouted and looked from Maria to Michael and on to Lily. "It's not like the mother is going to name him."

Lily walked over and handed the forms to Tracy, who was going to bring it back to the judge to sign. "That's true, but the baby is being placed in a foster home right out of the hospital and if all goes as planned the foster parents will be adopting him. I think they should name this baby since they're going to adopt him."

Michael nodded. "It makes sense."

Tracy frowned but said nothing further.

By the time the judge had signed all the orders, it was nearly five o'clock. "What do you say we call it a day and head over to Mulcahy's?" said Maria. She and Lily were the only ones left in the courtroom. "I've got something to tell you."

"Sure, but just a quick one," said Lily. "I've got responsibilities at home."

"What?" Maria looked confused. "I thought—"

Lily grinned. "Sam," she said. "Remember my dog? Michael's brothers watch him during the day, but I don't want to take advantage. Maybe they've got lives to live and places to be."

Maria nodded. "Yeah, I expect Michael does, or at least he used to." Then, after looking around the empty courtroom as if to make sure no one was listening, glanced at Lily. "Lately he hasn't been the same man about town."

"What do you mean?" asked Lily.

Maria shrugged and lowered her voice again, glancing around the room before she continued. "It's hard to put my finger on it, but things are different. There used to be a girl from Bayonne but that's been over for a while and I don't think there's anyone new on the scene." She rubbed the back of her neck and stretched. "And his relationship with Tracy has changed." She shook her head. "They are not as tight as they used to be." She stood up. "But we're wasting valuable time here. Let's get ourselves over to Mulcahy's before you start feeling guilty and run home. I do need to talk to you."

Although Mulcahy's was crowded they managed to find two empty stools. After they ordered their beers, Maria turned to Lily. "Are you doing anything this Saturday?"

Lily shook her head and grinned. "My social calendar is pretty clear these days."

"Want to come to a party?"

"Sure," said Lily. She liked Maria and was curious about her life and her little girl. She might even get to meet the boyfriend.

"Joe will be there," said Maria, "and a few other friends." She cleared her throat and looked a bit uncomfortable. "I've decided to marry him," she quickly added.

Lily smiled. "Congratulations! When's the big day?"

"In a couple of weeks and I hope you can make it, which is one reason why I thought it would be nice to have you meet Joe before then."

"Yeah, definitely. So you're engaged!" She looked down at Maria's bare hands. "Ring?"

Maria grinned sheepishly. "I think he's bringing it

over on Saturday night. He said something that made me think he was making a big deal about this."

"You sure I won't be barging in on a romantic evening?"

"Don't worry. For one thing, he invited his brother whom I've only met once, and another couple who are also old friends of mine. Then, of course, there's my mother, father, my daughter, and"—she shook her head and sighed—"if my mother gets wind of the fact that Joe may be bringing me a ring, she'll have the whole neighborhood there too."

"Sounds like a party," said Lily taking another sip of her beer. "Can I bring anything?"

"I guess it is," said Maria, "but there's no need to bring anything. When my mother is involved, there's always more than enough of everything."

Lily shrugged. "Okay, but be sure and give me directions. I don't want to be late and I still get hopelessly lost in Paterson except around here." She took one last sip of beer before she got up and pulled on her coat. "I better get going before Michael's brothers give up on me." She turned to Maria. "By the way, not sure what you meant about Michael back there in the courtroom."

Maria shrugged. "After he broke up with his girlfriend, which was about six months ago, he was out all the time." She pulled on her coat. "For a while I even wondered if he had something going with Tracy, they were so tight. Now I don't see any of that." She paused as she glanced at the papers she was putting into her briefcase. "Not that it's my business, but I think something's up with him. There is a difference in the way he acts. If I didn't know better, I'd almost think there was something going on between the two of you," she added, "but I know you're taken." She grinned. "Though you have to admit, he's very cute."

Lily arched an eyebrow and didn't say anything. There was no question that Michael was cute. She would even go so far to say that he was downright handsome with the best blue eyes, fine features, and a great body to boot. But she couldn't afford to be interested. She worked with him and besides, she was supposed to be committed to Josh. Right now though, she was very confused. Should she even be noticing Michael? If she was really committed to Josh, would she be aware of how attractive Michael was? Lately she'd been plagued by these doubts, but Lily wasn't prepared to talk about it and even if she was, Maria had enough on her mind with the upcoming wedding. She shouldn't have to be worrying about Lily and her unseemly attraction to Michael.

When she got to the house Patrick and Anthony were just finishing up. She was relieved that Michael wasn't there and irritated that Maria's conjectures and her own resulting thoughts had made her dread running into him. She'd liked things just the way they'd been with Michael and his brothers. Now she was afraid she'd suddenly feel self-conscious and spoil everything.

"You're just in time," said Patrick. "We're due at Ma's in ten minutes and she doesn't like it when we're late."

Anthony grinned. "Can you believe it? We're three grown men and yet we're still afraid to displease our mother. The woman's a tyrant."

"She's not so bad," said Michael, walking into the room, "just a bit demanding." He glanced at Lily. "Speaking of which, we're still on for Sunday, right?"

"Sure," she said. "Still planning on picking me up at two?" Lily asked. She didn't like the fact that she could almost feel her pulse speed up when he entered the room. Even in his uniform, it was obvious he was in great shape and now, at the end of the day, his easy smile that reached his vivid blue eyes stirred up something in the pit of her stomach. She hoped her voice and manner did not give her away because it would be very unprofessional of her to have anything but a friendly interest in the man.

"If that suits you," said Michael, apparently oblivious to his effect on her. "I'm free all day."

They agreed that two worked for both of them and the three brothers quickly departed, mumbling affectionate comments about their tyrannical mother. Lily was very intrigued to meet the woman.

Lily put the leash on Sam and led him downstairs. She realized that she was looking forward to an evening by herself. She had a nice bottle of white wine in the fridge and there might be a chunk of cheese in there somewhere and even some crackers. She would put some music on—starting with John Mayer. She planned to sit out in her garden and enjoy her new space. Even though it was October, the evening was warm.

It wasn't until she reached the bottom step that she saw him. Josh was just getting out of a cab in front of the house. She stopped short and stared. "What are you doing here?" she asked.

He turned and grinned. "Surprised to see me?"

Was she ever. She stood there, frozen, not believing her eyes while Sam pulled on his leash trying to get over and greet Josh. It had only been a month since she'd seen him, and she hadn't expected him until Thanksgiving at the earliest. "What are you doing here?" she repeated.

His smile started to slip. "Aren't you happy to see me?"

She shook her head. The man had come all this way to surprise her and she didn't know how she felt. It must be the unexpectedness of it, she decided. "Of course I'm happy," she said quickly. "It's just I can't believe it. I wasn't expecting you. I am in shock," she added, conscious that she was babbling.

"I thought it would be a good idea. It feels like it's been too long. When I found out that I had the weekend off, I looked online and they had cheap flights. So here I am."

He stood there staring at her for a moment, neither of them saying a word. Finally he spoke. "Can I come in?"

"Of course!" she said, noting from his tone that Josh wasn't sure of his welcome. What was happening here? She had to snap out of this and act excited! And it wasn't an act. She *was* excited, right?

She motioned for him to follow her through the door. Only then did it occur to her that they hadn't even kissed. She stopped abruptly and turned and smiled. "Welcome," she said. "I am really glad to see you. I'm just surprised."

He nodded but he still looked worried.

She felt bad.

"Maybe the surprise thing wasn't a good idea," he said.

"Don't be silly," she said as she walked into the apartment and turned on the front light. She knew she sounded insincere, but she didn't know how to change that. Instead, she leaned over in his direction so he could give her a peck on the cheek and an awkward hug.

"It's just that it has been a while," he repeated.

"I agree," she said quickly. "It's not good to be separated for so long."

Things didn't improve. In spite of herself, Lily felt cramped by Josh's presence. She didn't like it that Josh made himself at home or that he hung up his clothes in one of her closets. Even though he was not a particularly large person, he felt too big and too intrusive. It also didn't help that she had no food in the house and had not planned on making dinner.

"I'll cook," she said brightly. He'd come all this way, it was the least she could do. "Just give me a minute to run to the store and pick up some groceries."

Josh started to protest, but only halfheartedly and besides, Lily knew her man. He never liked to go out to dinner so he'd expect her to cook. The fact that he did was one of their issues, an issue she knew that would have to be dealt with if they were to make this relationship permanent, but now was not the time.

She pulled on her jacket and grabbed her wallet and headed for the door explaining that she was going to the corner store. She would pick up a chicken, some Spanish rice, and some vegetables. She could cook the chicken and rice together and throw together a salad. He couldn't expect more on a Friday night after a long day at the office.

When she got back and found him stretched out on her bed watching the television, she bit her tongue. It's not as if she had another place for him to sit. She still didn't have any furniture. And they were practically engaged. But for some reason she felt violated and intruded upon. He looked up when she walked in. "Nice place you've got here," he said, "though it's a bit small. How's the neighborhood?"

"Great," she said brightly, wondering how they were going to get through the weekend. "How long are you staying?"

"Only until Sunday morning," he said. "I'm on Sunday night so I've got to get back and there's no direct connection."

He came all the way just to see her. She felt guilty and miserable. They were supposed to be in a committed relationship. She knew that. She didn't want to have doubts. But if she were honest, she would have to admit that she wasn't happy to see him. But what should she do? They had been together six years. Would it be insane to talk about her doubts? Would it lead to a breakup? Is that what she wanted? She tried to tell herself it was very shortsighted of her to be so impatient with him. Everyone had ups and downs and doubts in their relationships. Right?

"Do you have any idea about what you'd like to do while you're here?" she asked, thinking that she wouldn't have to cancel with Michael on Sunday or explain about him either. She tried not to feel as if she were betraying Josh by worrying about Michael. She wanted to believe that Michael was nothing to her and she had done nothing wrong. But though she knew she had done nothing wrong, she wasn't so sure that Michael meant nothing to her. If he did then why did her heart beat faster every time Michael entered the room?

Josh looked puzzled. "What do I want to do? See you of course. Spend time with you."

She nodded. "Sure, but anything else?" She sighed, realizing that she needed to feel more amorous and not so tired.

He shook his head. "I just want to be with you."

His words did nothing for her and that confused her. Wasn't she in a romantic relationship with Josh? Where was her enthusiasm? She should be thrilled.

By the time Saturday afternoon rolled around Lily was losing her mind. Things were very tense with Josh but she couldn't seem to make the tension disappear. Everything he did annoyed her and she couldn't make herself ignore her feelings. Her annoyance extended to their physical relationship, what little there was. She didn't miss his kisses and didn't want them now. What was wrong with her?

She was very glad they had plans for Saturday night. She'd called Maria, who was thrilled that Lily was going to bring Josh to her party. She couldn't say that Josh was so thrilled. As he explained, he'd come to see her and not her new friends. But Lily explained—patiently, she thought—that they were part of her new life and Josh should know them.

Just as she feared, Lily and Josh were late getting to Maria's house although she didn't feel it was entirely her fault. While it was true that Lily always had trouble being on time, the main reason they were late was that they'd gotten lost in downtown Paterson. Maria's directions had seemed clear when she gave them to Lily, but as Josh and Lily circled the blocks, retracing their steps again and again, it felt as if Maria had given them a puzzle to solve. Getting lost didn't help Josh's mood. In the best of times he hated being late and hated not knowing where he was going even more, but in this instance he was on completely unfamiliar territory.

"I can't believe you're doing this to me," he said.

"What am I doing to you?" asked Lily, knowing full well what he was talking about, but she too was irritated and couldn't resist baiting him.

"Making me go to parties where I don't know anyone. My life is stressful enough. I don't need to come all the way out here to drive around in circles and get lost so I can go to a party where I won't know a soul."

Lily didn't answer. While what he said irritated her there was also a grain of truth in his words. She knew how he felt about things like this—that he hated parties unless they were given and attended by close friends; and foremost, that he hated being late. She almost felt guilty and wondered if she was being unfair to him, putting him in this situation.

But when Maria opened the door and pulled Lily and

Josh into her apartment and with her arm around them both brought them over to meet her parents, Lily forgot about any of that. Both of Maria's parents smiled up at her and Maria's father held out his hand. "I am so pleased to meet you," he said. "I feel as if I've already known you because Maria talks so much about you."

Maria's mother nodded.

"She doesn't speak much English," explained Maria, "but she understands plenty."

"It's very nice to meet both of you," said Lily. "I'm so happy to be included in this celebration."

Maria's mother's eyes lit up. "Celebration," she said. "It is a time for joy."

Maria sighed and shook her head. "She's over the top that I'm finally going to get married."

Maria's mother beamed.

Lily looked around the room full of people of all ages, all talking at once.

Maria lived on the second floor of a two-family house. Maria's father explained that he and Maria's mother lived on the floor below, making it convenient for them to watch Isabelle. Maria's apartment consisted of a fairly large front room that Maria used for a living room, opening into another large room that was the dining room. The kitchen was next, right behind the dining room, and the bedrooms, Lily assumed, were off the kitchen. Both front rooms, as well as the kitchen, were filled with people. Latin music was blaring and the dining room table was covered with platters piled high with food.

"Come on," said Maria. "Let me take you over to meet Joe."

They made their way across the crowded room to where Joe was talking to some people. He was about five feet ten and good-looking with dark black hair and dark eyes. He smiled and put out his hand when they were introduced. Lily extended hers. "Congratulations," she said.

He beamed. "Thank you," he said, shaking her hand. "I'm very glad to meet you. Maria is very happy to have you as a partner in court."

"That's nice to hear," Lily said. "I also enjoy working with her."

Maria extended her hand and smiled. "What do you think?"

Lily took Maria's hand and admired the ring. "Beautiful," she said. Then she turned to Joe. "You did a good job."

He grinned. "Thank God! I feared for my life that I'd screw up. Now we just have to pick a date and find a place."

"We've got a band," Maria explained. "One of Joe's good friends will do that as a wedding gift. And I've already checked with the church. They gave me a couple of dates for next month. I've just got to check with some of the halls and restaurants around here to see what is available. It shouldn't be that difficult to get the rest of it organized."

Lily grinned and shook her head. Maria had to be the most relaxed bride she'd ever met. Most people needed at least a year to plan a wedding; just look at Tracy. And here was Maria who would probably get it all done in a month.

She glanced over at Josh to see what he made of all this wedding stuff, but he'd disappeared. She started to look for him until Joe explained that he'd gone into the back room. "The Yankees are playing," he said, "and it's close."

They didn't get home until after one. There'd been eating, dancing, and much conversation. Even when she left at twelve thirty, the party was going strong, but the game had ended and Josh reminded her that he had an early flight the next day. The only way he could get back in time for evening rounds was to book a connecting flight through Chicago that left at ten.

Because they both had a good time at the party, the tension between them had vanished and Lily felt more conciliatory.

"I hope you didn't mind going," she began. "Maybe it wasn't how you would have wanted to spend the weekend."

He shrugged. "I actually had fun. I hardly ever get to see the Yankees on TV and it was an exciting game." There were a few minutes of silence and then he reached over and squeezed her hand. "I probably should have called before I came out here," he said quietly. "You've made a life for yourself here and I wasn't taking that into account."

She didn't respond, but instead vowed she'd make things right between them when they got back to the apartment. She knew him well enough to know that it wasn't easy for him to acknowledge that he wasn't perfect. Besides, every relationship had its ups and downs and she thought she might have been a bit unfair to Josh this weekend.

But her plan to make amends was thwarted, for when she came out of the bathroom after washing her face, Josh had fallen sound asleep, fully clothed, on top of the covers.

"Poor baby," she murmured as she loosened his shirt and pulled a blanket over him. "This was all too much for you."

The next morning she was awakened by Josh softly calling her name. "I already walked the dog, so don't worry about him." She sat up and rubbed her eyes. Josh was standing before her with his jacket on and his suitcase in hand.

"I've got to go," he said, "or I'll miss my flight."

She started to get up. "I can drive you," she said.

He shook his head. "I already called a cab." He paused. "Listen, sorry I fell asleep last night. I guess I needed the sleep too." There was another awkward moment of silence. Josh cleared his throat. "Next time, let's meet in a neutral place. I think that might work better."

She nodded. She doubted that a change of venue would change things between them. On the other hand, it had been six years. Shouldn't they at least try and make it work?

Josh quickly kissed her good-bye and was gone.

After he left, Lily felt guilty and confused. Josh came all the way to see her and they had hardly connected.

She'd been more concerned about going to Maria's party than making him happy. What kind of a woman was she? Did they just need more time alone together so she'd remember why it was that she cared about him? Or had she stopped loving him and no change of venue or thoughtfulness on her part would change that?

But now was not the time to wonder. Michael was coming over to pick her up and show her the buildings he was considering. As it was, she was running late and was just about to blow-dry her hair when Michael arrived and she answered the door wearing a bathrobe and a soaking wet head.

"Don't rush on my account," said Michael, looking her up and down and grinning. "Has the dog been walked?" he added when Sam came bounding out.

"A while ago," she said. "I'm sure he'd be happy for another walk, especially since I'm going to be leaving him for a while."

"Let me take him out while you finish getting ready."

She gratefully agreed, glad that some things weren't complicated, and went back into her bedroom. When she returned twenty minutes later she found him settled in the kitchen, looking very much at ease at her kitchen table with a cup of coffee and the Sunday paper.

"Sam's been walked and Patrick said he'll come by later so he'll get out again." He glanced over at her, again giving her the once-over. From the look on his face, it seemed that he approved of her short corduroy skirt, leather boots, and suede jacket.

"All set?" he said after a pause.

She nodded and tried to ignore how good he looked

in his jeans and a blue chambray shirt that he wore under a worn brown leather flight jacket. She told herself that Michael was uncomplicated and they were just friends, nothing more. With that thought firmly implanted in her brain, she managed to calm down and focus on what he was saying.

"What I'd like to do," he said as he opened the door to the passenger side of his Jeep and waited for Lily to get in before closing it, "is to take you to our other building that's completed except for the fixtures and paint. Pat said you really have an eye for color."

She nodded. "I think he might be exaggerating my ability, but I'm happy to give my opinion."

Michael shook his head and shrugged. "Don't think so. You always look great and your apartment already looks like something out of a magazine, so I'm sure he wasn't."

She didn't say anything, though she was thrilled to hear his words. She liked to think she had style, but her job as a lawyer for the state didn't give her a lot of opportunity to express it.

He turned down a street and slowed down to look for a space to park. "Are you on a schedule today?"

"Not really," she said. She was meeting Arlene for dinner in Hoboken at six so she had plenty of time.

"Good because I'd like to drive you around down here and show you some of the buildings we're considering. We've got bids on two and there's a third we're considering. I could use a second opinion."

"Sure," she said. "I'd be happy to, but it's not like I'm qualified—I just enjoy it."

He shook his head. "You're being too modest. It's more than that. I think you have a good feel and you have a better idea than we do about what people want."

She shrugged.

"How long did you live in Hoboken?"

"A few years."

"Anywhere else?"

"Boston for college, Baltimore before that."

He nodded. "As I said, you are a lot more qualified than the three of us. Both those cities and Hoboken too have been gentrified. That's what's happening here in Jersey City. You've seen what it should look like. We've lived here all our lives."

She shrugged. "When you put it like that I can't argue. Besides," she added, "it's fun and I do like houses."

Chapter Nine

The first building was only around the corner from Lily's apartment. It was also a brownstone, but this time the brothers had divided the original one-family house into two duplexes. "We've still got to landscape the outside," said Michael, pointing to the sad-looking square of yard filled with dead shrubs and litter as he led Lily into the first floor though the iron gate. "But we've already started on the garden out back."

The layout of the apartment was similar to Lily's, except for the two additional bedrooms on the second floor. Because all the windows faced north and the building itself was surrounded by high-rises, the first-floor apartment was darker. Michael directed her into the space that would be the kitchen.

She looked around, taking in the large empty square room and tried to envision what it would be like once it was filled with appliances and cabinets and had a real floor. "You're going to want good lighting," she said, "and everything needs to be in light colors."

He picked up the red Spanish tile and handed it to her with a grin. "I take it that this won't do."

She shook her head, determined to stay focused on the task at hand, and not on the fact that she found his grin infectious and sexy. What kind of woman found a man sexy only hours after her significant other had left? She turned from him and walked over to look at the other samples. After a minute or so she found what she was looking for and handed him a light salmon-colored tile. "This might work."

He nodded and laid it on the counter.

"Show me sample cabinet veneers," she said, "and we'll see which ones go best."

Michael pointed to a pile of wood chips on another counter and Lily rummaged through them until she found one that she liked. She laid the sample next to the tile on the counter and moved back a few feet, studying it as she did. Finally, she nodded with satisfaction. "This'll work fine." She looked around the dark space. "Even so, you've got to use white or even chrome appliances and both overhead and undermounted lighting."

Michael winced. "All that lighting is going to cost money. Is it really necessary?"

She shrugged. "You're the boss. I'm just telling you what I think would work best."

He looked around the dark room and back at her, this time with a look of resignation. "I'll price it out, and unless it's totally outrageous, I'll do as you say."

She looked around the room. "Couldn't you save money somewhere else? Maybe use less expensive cabinets?"

He shrugged. "I guess I could." He glanced at his watch and then grabbed her by the hand. "I'd like to get through this building quickly so we have time at the end to show you the ones I'm thinking about buying."

They moved fast, assessing the bathrooms to decide if he could use the same tile that he'd used in her building. She almost didn't have time to think about the fact that Michael had held her hand. Not until they were back in the Jeep headed for the next building. Michael was concentrating on maneuvering through the one-way streets that surrounded the square so she had a minute to herself. She reminded herself that she and Josh had been dating for six years. That had to count for something. Besides that, she worked with Michael, and most importantly, she had no idea what he thought of her. Any attraction between them could be just one-sided and if she ever mentioned it, he might think she was crazy. He had never given any indication of anything but friendship, though she certainly hadn't indicated anything on her part. That he'd grabbed her hand probably had more to do with their comfort level and his obvious impatience with the time it was taking to pick out colors than any kind of feelings for her. The only thing she was sure of was that he wanted a second opinion about the buildings he was thinking about, and she was flattered that he cared about what she thought.

"So tell me," she said as they slowly drove through the narrow streets in search of a parking space close to the next building, "how does this renovation business fit into being a sheriff in a courtroom?"

He looked over at her and grinned sheepishly. "Weird, huh?"

She nodded and then waited as he slowed down in front of a space, not speaking until he'd carefully backed into to it and turned off the engine. He turned and faced her. "I put myself through college working construction. I worked for a guy putting up apartment buildings on the waterfront in Hoboken. I hadn't been doing it very long before I realized that I liked it. Liked working with my hands and liked the whole idea of designing and building something. At the same time I was watching the neighborhood. I grew up pretty close to here and I could see what was going on. Gentrification has been really slow in Jersey City, but it's been going on for about fifteen years."

They got out of the car and walked down the street to the next building. Michael continued to talk as they went. "During the summer before my senior year, I spotted a building that was for sale. It was a real wreck and needed a lot of work, but it was in a decent neighborhood. I thought it had a lot of potential. I wanted to buy it and fix it up, but I knew I couldn't do it alone, not if I was going to school. I talked to my brothers. Anthony was still in high school then and Patrick was in his freshman year at Rutgers. They were game. Then I went to my mother. At first she thought I was nuts. After a lot of convincing we worked out a deal. She'd lend me the money if I got a secure job with the city or the state— one with benefits, pensions, job security, the whole nine yards." He paused. "She made the same deal with my brothers when they got out." He turned and grinned at her. "Which is why I'm a court sheriff, Pat's a fireman, and Anthony works for transit."

She must have looked surprised. "Pat and Anthony, but they're always at the site."

He nodded. "They work nights and weekends, which is why they're around during the day."

She grinned and shook her head. "Now I'm beginning to understand."

Michael stopped in front of a two-story clapboard house stuck between two brownstones. She looked at it closely. Unlike the brownstones that dominated the neighborhood, this house, besides having a wooden frame, was much smaller. Instead of the steep front steps that most brownstones had, the front door of this house was on the street level. "This used to be a one-family house," Michael explained as he unlocked the front door. "The same family lived in it from 1790 until about 1955 when it was sold. By then the neighborhood had deteriorated and it was turned into a rooming house." He closed the door behind him.

Lily was enchanted from the moment she walked into the two-story foyer. Light streamed in from the second-story windows so that the room was bright even before Michael turned on the tarnished chandelier that was hanging from the ceiling. Again taking her by the hand, he led her from room to room, not saying a word. Lily felt as if he was leading her through a museum full of masterpieces or a world famous cathedral, such was his reverence. And she had to agree with him.

Even though the rooms were dingy and in desperate need of paint and the scale of the rooms was much smaller than anything they'd already seen, it was obvious that the place was a treasure. Each room had almost floor-to-ceiling windows that made the house much brighter. She walked into the front parlor on the first floor and immediately noticed that most of the original woodwork was still intact. Michael saw her looking at it and explained that he intended to keep all the moldings and beautifully carved woodwork. "They chopped up some of the house," he said. "You'll see when we get up to the second floor, so we'll have to replace moldings and door frames, but down here everything is pretty much intact. We should be able to completely restore it by replacing what was removed. What we can't find, we can make. Anthony is the best at woodworking and he's gotten good at repairing and replacing."

Since Michael said he wasn't ready to do the kitchen on this house—he was thinking of hiring an architect so it could be done just right—it didn't take Lily long to pick out tiles and fixtures for the bathroom. Light was not an issue, and her main concern was that what she chose not be oversized or ornate. Within a half hour they were back in the car. Michael glanced over at her after looking down at his watch. "It's three thirty," he said. "You up for seeing those buildings I was telling you about?"

She nodded. "You've got me curious." She still had a couple of hours before she had to go back and change. And she was having a good time.

He grinned. "Thanks. You'll be a help, especially

now that you've seen our other places." Michael called the broker, who agreed to meet them at the first building only a few blocks away. Both buildings were in walking distance of each other and Lily's apartment, so they drove back to Lily's block, parked the truck, and proceeded on foot.

"So what happened to the first building that you bought?" Lily asked.

"That's where my brothers and I live," he said and then grinned before adding, "and my mother and my uncle and my cousin." He looked over at her and smiled. "It's a pretty big building."

She only nodded, not sure what she thought about a building filled with Frascatos.

"Needless to say, my mother doesn't pay rent and my uncle and cousin don't pay market. But the building is ours and has increased in value every year we've owned it."

"Have you found another tenant for my building?"

He shook his head. "The apartment isn't quite done, but we should start doing something about that."

She nodded. "And this time you'll have a lease for the tenant to sign."

He reached over and brushed a strand of hair off her face before answering. "You're probably thinking we need someone to handle the business end of the operation."

She shrugged, "Well, at least to cover the basics." She tried not to think about how much she liked how she felt when he touched her or even the fact that he had. He probably wasn't even aware of it.

"I don't disagree. It just never occurred to us. And up until now it's worked fine. We got to do what we wanted. We all have other incomes and the buildings are appreciating so who cares." He glanced sideways at her to see if she was going to interrupt. She said nothing. "I promise. Whoever rents it will have a lease."

"And you'll charge market value?"

He nodded and gave her a crooked grin. "From now on."

"And me?"

He looked puzzled.

"I doubt I pay market."

He shrugged. "Maybe not, but so what? Sam keeps my brothers company and your input is invaluable."

It was her turn to grin.

Both brownstones that they looked at needed a lot of work, but one had never been broken up for apartments. Like the previous house, the same family had lived in the house since it had been built. This house was built in the 1880s and the last surviving member had died only recently. The house had long been neglected, but as Michael explained when they left the broker, "It's a lot easier to fix something that's been neglected than if it's been chopped up and reconfigured."

The other building was broken up into ten apartments. The building needed some work, but probably could be in habitable condition within a few months.

"So what'd you think?" asked Michael as they walked back to her apartment.

"They were great, especially the one-family. It could be stunning. And the other one could really make you some money." She grinned and nudged him. "Especially if you charged market."

He smiled. "I will. Promise. The rest of my relatives have places to live so they won't be coming to me." He stopped in front of her building and turned to her. "I'd like to be able to buy both buildings, but it's going to mean more work for all of us and more of a time commitment."

"Do you intend to keep working as a sheriff?"

"That's the question," he said shaking his head. "In two years I qualify for a pension so maybe I should stay until then. On the other hand," he added, "more would happen if I committed to renovating these buildings."

"What about your mother?"

"What do you mean?"

"What would she say?"

He shrugged. "She'd probably like me to stay and vest in my pension, but at this point she understands that she has no say." He glanced over at her. "I did what she asked when I borrowed money from her, but that was over eight years ago. That money has all been paid back. She can tell me to be on time when she has me over for dinner, but not what to do with my life."

"I see," she said. She was happy to hear that.

Michael glanced at his watch. "It's five o'clock. Do you want to get some dinner?"

She shook her head with regret, since she had plans. She explained that she was going to meet up with some friends in Hoboken. What she didn't tell him was that meeting Arlene for dinner was probably the last thing that she wanted to do. But she'd made a commitment.

Besides, maybe it was just as well. Michael was very attractive and even more appealing as she got to know him. But they worked together. Today had been great—no, wonderful—she corrected herself. She had really enjoyed his company. But she was involved with Josh. Going out with Michael probably would have come to nothing, but she didn't think she should take the chance.

Chapter Ten

On Monday Lily received a call from Irene, the supervising caseworker. "We've got a problem," she began. "Remember the Romano family?"

Lily did. It was one of the first cases she'd had upon coming to the Paterson office. The DYFS was involved because Mr. Romano had been abusing his wife and had even threatened to kill her and their kids. One of the children reported that he'd chased them around the house with a carving knife. Mrs. Romano couldn't protect herself or stand up to her husband and denied that anything was going on. However, family members had called the police and although Mr. Romano had denied the allegations, the kids had backed up one another's stories. Mr. Romano was arrested and, as far as Lily knew, incarcerated.

"Not anymore," said Irene. "He was released from

jail last week and is back home. We got a call from Mrs. Romano's sister," she explained.

"She let him back in," asked Lily, "after what he did?"

"Yeah," said Irene. "Some women just don't get it. You should know that."

Lily sighed. "I suppose. But I can't believe, after the way he was with those kids, that she would let him in."

"She says he has nowhere else to go."

"Unless she's willing to go to a shelter with her kids, it looks like we should remove them," said Lily.

"Do you think the court will go along with that?" asked Irene.

"At least we can try," said Lily. "I'll call the court and get a time when we can come in. You call Mrs. Romano and tell her that we're going to be making an application to the court to remove the children. Mr. Romano can come too if he wants."

Tracy told Lily that the court would hear her motion at one thirty that day.

Lily called Irene and gave her the time. She also called Maria to let her know what was happening. Maria explained that she already had an appointment in the afternoon to see some children on her caseload. "Fill me in," she said. "If I agree with your position, would it be okay if I appeared by phone?"

Lily would have preferred to have Maria's support but understood how important it was that she see her clients. After she filled Maria in on the situation, Maria concurred and they agreed she would appear by phone unless the judge objected.

Lily called Irene back to discuss the case. "Why

don't you try and get Mrs. Romano to leave her husband," Lily said, "so we don't have to ask for the kids' removal." She hated taking kids from their parents. But it was a necessary evil if the parents were going to place them in danger. "Maybe Mrs. Romano's sister would agree to take them until Mrs. Romano could be convinced that it was in her and her children's best interests to keep Mr. Romano out of the house. In the meantime, we can see if Mr. Romano is willing to cooperate. We can give him a chance. We'll ask the judge to order a psychological evaluation and also ask that Romano attend anger management. I don't know about you," she said to Irene, "but I'm not too optimistic that he'll cooperate, but we're obligated by law to try." Her recollection of Romano was that he was not open to suggestions or change. She suspected he saw his wife and his children as extensions of himself and not as individuals who needed to be respected.

When Lily got to the courtroom at one fifteen, the first person she saw was Michael. "Did you see your guy out there?" he asked.

Lily shook her head. "I'm not sure. Was he sitting on the bench in the hallway?"

Michael nodded. "He's the one in the black leather jacket. His wife was next to him." He shook his head. "Some attitude," he murmured.

Her heart sank. She hoped this wasn't going to get ugly.

"To be on the safe side, I'm going to call for some backup," Michael said.

Irene was waiting for her inside the courtroom.

"Michael told me to come in here," she said, "after Mr. Romano gave me a hard time."

Tracy poked her head out. "Judge wants to know if you're ready."

Lily nodded. "We're set to go." She figured they should do this quickly before Romano had any more time to heat up.

Michael brought in the Romanos and directed them to sit at the table on the left side of the courtroom in front of the judge's bench and across from the table where Lily was sitting with Irene. The judge walked in moments later with Michael's announcement that all rise. Lily and Irene, and the Romanos, after a moment's hesitation, stood until the judge sat down and motioned for everyone to be seated.

Judge Keegan turned to Lily. "Ms. Hanson, what have you got for me today?"

Lily explained about Mr. Romano getting out of jail and coming home to his wife in violation of the restraining order that had been issued.

"Don't these parties have attorneys?" asked the judge.

Lily shook her head. "At the last hearing, Mr. Romano said they didn't need lawyers. He said he'd done nothing wrong and didn't understand why he had to be here."

The judge turned to Mr. Romano. "Is it still the case that you do not want a lawyer or have you reconsidered?"

"Why should I get a lawyer?"

The judge shook his head. "You're entitled to counsel. If you can't afford a lawyer, the court will appoint one for you."

Romano shook his head. "I don't want a lawyer.

What I do want is for these people to get out of my life. All I want to do is go home to my family. Why are they interfering?"

Lily looked over at Mrs. Romano and knew that they wouldn't be getting help from her. Her head bent, she didn't look at anyone. Her arms were folded in front of her as if protecting herself from invasion. She couldn't protect herself, much less her kids. It was going to have to be up to Lily.

The judge looked at Lily. "Ms. Hanson?"

She launched into her argument. "Judge, Mr. Romano is in violation of a restraining order that was filed because he threatened his wife and his children with a carving knife. It has also been alleged that he physically abused Mrs. Romano. Before he returns to the home we are asking that he have a psychological evaluation and follow the recommendations. We are also asking that he attend classes in anger management. DYFS will schedule both the psychological and the classes."

The judge looked at Mr. Romano. "Do you understand what she's saying? If you get the evaluation and start the classes you probably can go back in the home—that is, if you get good reports."

"But it's my house. I have my rights." He paused and shook his head. "Besides, I have nowhere else to go."

The judge sighed and turned to Lily. "Any response, Counselor?"

"Right now he's in violation of a restraining order. If he has the psychological and goes to the classes, the restraining order can be lifted. Otherwise, he's going to have to go back to jail."

The judge looked over at Mr. Romano. "Well?"

"It's my house," repeated Romano. "I'm not leaving it." He suddenly got to his feet. "I won't be pushed around by that one over there," he snarled, pointing to Lily. "No one tells me what to do."

Even from where he stood, she could feel his anger focused on her and every time he raised his voice she felt as if she'd been punched, but she stood her ground. She wasn't going to back down. Suddenly she realized that two more sheriffs had joined Michael in the courtroom. One stood directly behind Romano, the other to his right, between Lily and his wife. Michael stood right behind Lily. She realized that when he leaned toward Romano and told him to watch his mouth.

The judge looked down from the bench and glowered at Romano. "Any more remarks like that and you'll be spending the night in jail for contempt." He paused before continuing, "No one is trying to strong-arm you. However, you are already in violation of a restraining order by being in your home with your family. If you want to live with them, you must do what the Deputy Attorney General has asked." He locked eyes with Mr. Romano. "Unless you want to get locked up again, find somewhere else to live. Leave peacefully and make arrangements with the caseworker for the evaluation and counseling." He started to stand up. "We'll see you back here in two months. We should have the results of the evaluation and you should have started your counseling sessions by then. At that time we'll decide whether you can return to your family."

The judge left the bench and Lily stood up and turned

to Irene. "Take Mr. Romano outside and give him the dates and address where he's to go for his appointments." Lily looked over at him and then lowered her voice. "Make sure one of the sheriffs is with you. If he gives you a hard time, come back in here immediately."

Irene nodded and followed the Romanos out of the courtroom. Lily turned back to the table where she'd left her papers and bag. She took several deep breaths. Michael was still standing there.

"You okay?" he asked.

She nodded and gave him a half smile, finding herself grateful that he'd been there to protect her, and realizing that now that the man was out of the courtroom and away from her, she'd been scared. She looked up at Michael. "The guy is his own worst enemy." She shook her head. "He's not going to get back in the house unless he does what's ordered."

Michael frowned. "I'm not so sure. I think he's a lot more dangerous than our usual. There's only so much that the courts can do."

Lily grimaced, hoping Michael wasn't right about him being so dangerous. Irene was also at risk, as were his wife and kids. "You certainly had him covered in here," she said.

Michael nodded. "You can never be too careful. Besides, one of those guys was fresh out of training and the other one comes to every emergent call we've got. He's always hoping for action." He grinned. "I'm not sure if I could have relied on either of them, but at least we looked strong."

Lily nodded. "It did seem to work. She turned and

looked back toward the door. "Since Irene isn't back, I hope that means Mr. Romano agreed to leave the house. Otherwise we've got to involve the police and have him arrested. If Mrs. Romano won't press charges, we'll have to remove the kids."

Michael moved as if to walk away and then turned back. "My mother wants you to come for dinner," he said in a rush.

"Really?"

Michael smiled and nodded. "Anthony and Patrick told her all about you and Sam. She wants to meet you both." He shook his head and shrugged. "What can I say? She has always wanted to know who our friends are."

Chapter Eleven

Maria called Lily at the office. "Don't make any plans for the fifth."

"Okay," said Lily. "What's up?"

"We've finally set the date," said Maria, her voice shrill with what Lily imagined must have been nervousness and excitement.

"You're getting married November 5?"

"Yeah," said Maria.

"But that's only a few weeks away," said Lily. "How did you find something that soon? Are you really ready?" Lily couldn't believe Maria would be able to pull the wedding together that quickly.

"To answer your first question, there was a cancellation and my dad is friends with the caterer. As for your second, of course I'm not ready. I haven't done anything yet!" She sounded as if she was gasping for air. "And I can't really take much time off. I've got too much to do here. Besides, I want to use the vacation I've got left for a honeymoon."

"A honeymoon?" Lily laughed. "One minute you're dragging your feet and the next, you're jumping in with both of them." She paused, trying to absorb Maria's news. It was obvious that Maria was very happy and Lily was glad for her. "Tell me everything," she said. "Start at the beginning, and when you're done, let me know what I can do to help."

Maria sighed again. "Oh, Lily, thanks for understanding and not making too much fun of me. I am excited; I can't help it. I keep looking at this ring and want to pinch myself. Can this really be happening to me?"

Lily smiled as she listened to her friend. "So where are you going on your honeymoon?"

"Promise not to laugh?"

"Of course not," said Lily crossing her fingers, hoping she wouldn't be tempted.

"Puerto Rico."

"So what's to laugh at?"

"It's so unadventurous. It's where we're both from. We'll spend the whole time visiting family."

"So go somewhere else."

"But I want to go there. I want them all to meet Joe."

"Oh." Lily could see that she was not going to get anywhere with Maria this morning. "So tell me how I can help." She figured she would leave the subject of the honeymoon alone. It clearly was too complicated for a nine a.m. chat.

"I want to adjourn everything we've got on for the last week of October and the first week of November."

"No one will cover for you?"

"I hate to ask for help. Besides, I prefer to do my own cases. What I was thinking was that we could do a double calendar when I get back. That way all the cases would be heard in a timely way."

Lily's ear didn't even register any longer that this was grammatically incorrect, since the term *timely* was so commonplace in her office.

"That's fine," she said. It would mean more work, but Lily was glad to accommodate her friend. She also knew Maria was uncomfortable having anyone represent her "babies" but her. "Let the judge know I have no objections to an adjournment."

"Thanks. You're the best."

"Anything else?"

"Just be there."

Lily smiled. "I wouldn't miss it for the world."

On Wednesday when Lily got home, Sam was not in the apartment. There was a note on the door saying that Pat had taken him upstairs to the third floor. Lily went up to get him. The brothers were just finishing when she arrived. As was his habit, Sam was lying on the floor halfway between the two men. He didn't even get up when he saw Lily, but wagged his tail and lifted his head in acknowledgment. He was, Lily knew, at least as attached to the brothers as he was to her. She hoped that they would take him along when they renovated the next building or else he'd be brokenhearted.

"We're almost finished with this apartment," said Patrick. "Want to look around?"

She nodded, taking in the living room that was freshly painted Navajo white. They had done a beautiful job.

"Come see the kitchen," said Anthony. "You were right about doing everything in white. Look how much brighter the room is."

The room did look good, particularly when she compared it to how it had been before they covered up the dingy hospital green paint from the prior owner.

"Have you rented the apartments yet?"

Patrick shook his head. "I think Michael's going to talk to you about that. We're wondering if we should use a broker or try renting them ourselves. Hate to pay the broker's commission."

"Yeah, but then you're protected some."

"What do you mean?"

"Well they pretty much weed out the people who can't afford to pay the rent by having them fill out references and stuff."

"We could do that," said Pat.

Lily nodded. "But would you?"

Pat shook his head and grinned. "You know us too well, but it's Michael that you should talk to."

"Talk to me about what?"

Michael had just walked into the apartment. He'd changed from his uniform into well-worn jeans and a red flannel shirt. He looked good. Lily couldn't help but smile at the sight of him, conscious of how happy she was to see him. *Had that always been the case?* she wondered. She couldn't exactly remember when she had started to become so fond of him and when she had begun to notice him.

"The apartments look terrific," she said, "and ready for tenants. I was just asking if you were going to use a broker."

He shrugged. "Do you think we should?" Michael smiled at Lily. "Don't you think we can spot deadbeats or deal with them if they are?"

She shook her head and grinned. "Once you've got someone in your apartment, they are hard to get rid of, even if they don't pay the rent."

Michael looked from one brother to the other and then shrugged. "I suppose we should, at least for this building and until we've had some experience."

Lily noticed an exchange pass between his two brothers.

Patrick shrugged. "Whatever you say. You're the boss."

Michael looked at Anthony. "Same here," said Anthony. "You know you always do what you want anyway."

Michael had the decency to look a little embarrassed. "I wouldn't go that far . . . ," he started to say and then, catching an exchange of looks between his brothers, smiled and shook his head. "Well, I am the oldest."

Lily nodded to Sam. "Let's go, boy," she said. "I think we need to leave these brothers in peace." Sam got to his feet and after slowly stretching, followed her to the door.

"Lily?" Michael asked. "Let me walk you downstairs. I wanted to talk to you about something."

"Sure," she said, noting another exchange of looks between the other two brothers. What were they picking up that she wasn't?

Michael turned back to them. "Want to meet me outside by the truck in about five?"

As they walked down the two flights, Michael asked her if she knew of any rental agents in Jersey City. She didn't, but promised she'd ask around her office the next day and let him know. "There's one more thing," Michael said, as she unlocked the door to her apartment. She turned and looked at him expectantly. "About dinner at Ma's—"

"Yeah?"

"Sunday?"

"Okay." She wondered what she was getting herself into.

"Pick you both up at five?"

"Sam too?"

"Absolutely. She really does want to meet him." He turned and opened the outside door and then looked back at her. "Oh, I almost forgot," he said. "There's something else," he said. "Maria called me today about her wedding."

Lily smiled and nodded. "She's very excited in spite of herself."

"He seems like a good guy," said Michael.

"You've met him?"

"Yeah, he was in Mulcahy's one night and then we all went out for dinner afterward."

"Ahh."

Michael leaned on the door frame. "Do you want to go together?" he asked.

"Together?" said Lily. Did he mean like a date? She

knew she couldn't do that. She and Josh may have problems but that would be cheating.

"Yeah, together. Like we both go in the same car since we're both coming from the same neighborhood. I thought it would be easier."

Lily smiled, trying to hide her relief. She could do that without feeling guilty and it meant she wouldn't have to deal with whatever was going on between her and Michael, at least not yet. "Sure," she said quickly. "That's a good idea. It would be much easier. You want me to drive?"

Michael grinned. "What's the matter? You don't think the Jeep quite makes it for special occasions?"

She tilted her head and rolled her eyes. "Well . . ."

"Maybe it would be a good idea to take your car," he said. "I might even let you drive." He winked to show he was kidding.

Before Lily had a chance to respond Michael had turned and headed for the front door. "See you then, unless you're back in court."

"Don't think so."

"Sunday then, dinner at Ma's."

She closed the door behind him and turned on some lights, conscious of the fact that she was very curious to meet Ma and that the prospect of Maria's wedding suddenly seemed brighter and more exciting than it had fifteen minutes earlier. Michael only invited her to dinner with his mother because his mother apparently liked to keep track of all his and his brothers' friends, and of course, she wanted to see her dog. He'd asked her to drive with him to the wedding because it was convenient. But it still would be fun to go to the wedding with Michael. She would have someone to talk to and maybe even dance with.

The message light was blinking. She shut her eyes and cringed. What if it was Josh? She did not want to hear it. It had been a long day and now she wanted to enjoy her privacy and think about what she'd wear to Maria's wedding. She walked over to the phone and took it off the hook, feeling only a twinge of guilt. It wasn't as if she didn't care for Josh, but it had been a rough day with a few shiny spots and right now she wanted to dwell on those. If she talked to him, he might bring her down.

Chapter Twelve

Lily woke up Saturday morning feeling energized. It was a sunny October day with the first sign of frost in the air. After taking Sam for a brisk walk through the neighborhood, she hurried back to her warm apartment. Wrapping her hands around her first cup of coffee, she sat in her living room looking out at her backyard and the mums she planted when she first moved in. Life was looking good. She liked her job and the people she worked with. She loved her apartment and even though she still had work to do on it, she thought, looking around at the still mostly empty space, the place had good bones and, even half-empty, felt good. Her plan that day was to go shopping in New York. She still had to buy things for her apartment and she needed to get a dress for Maria's wedding. She figured she couldn't afford any of the furniture she found in the City but would get lots of ideas. Looking at those apartments with Michael had been very stimulating and she had been thinking of what she could do with her own space as well as some of the spaces she'd seen with him. Today she planned to go down to Chelsea to ABC Carpet and see what was going on in the world of interior design. Then the following week she'd face budget realities and go to IKEA or one of those other warehouse stores and find a couch and maybe a coffee table.

And then there was the need for a dress for Maria's wedding. She smiled to herself. Of course she had something in her closet that would do. But the occasion seemed to demand a new dress—something fun. There were all kinds of little boutiques in Chelsea and the West Village from high-priced designers to some of the discount stores to vintage shops. The wedding was a few weeks away so she had time, and in the meantime, what would be the harm in looking to see what was out there?

Of course the fact that she was going with Michael hardly entered her head or affected her decision to look for a new dress. They were just friends and were only going together as a matter of convenience. The fact that he was attractive and that she was noticing that more and more didn't enter into her thinking. Nor did she let herself think too much about the fact that she was going over to his mother's house tomorrow for dinner. His mother liked dogs and she was a new friend of her sons. Maybe all Italian mothers were like that. On Sunday they made pasta and had to find someone to eat it. It did cross her mind that she might be being a little bit dishonest, but she wasn't quite sure what to do about that, so she pushed such thoughts to the back of her mind, at least for the time being.

She looked at her watch. She needed to talk to Josh. She hadn't spoken to him in two days. She felt a twinge, but wasn't sure if it was guilt or annoyance. She knew he wouldn't be happy with her once they finally did speak. Although it was his idea that they live apart and pursue their own dreams, he didn't like it when she was too independent. While it was assumed that he might not be home at night because of his work schedule, she found herself having to explain every social occasion of her own. When had he become so annoying, or had she overlooked his faults when they first began dating? She almost regretted that she'd taken the receiver off the hook the night before. But part of her was amused. It obviously was time that she stood up to him; in fact, it was long overdue. He needed to learn that sulking and guilt trips weren't okay. She'd been catering to him and his whims and moods for so long that she didn't have a clue as to how he'd react to her new show of independence. She was almost afraid to find out. Or was it simply that she really didn't care enough?

She looked at her watch. It was just about ten. If she left now and plugged in the phone just before she went out the door, he'd probably still be in bed out there in South Dakota and she wouldn't have to talk to him until she got back. She paused, wondering if she should feel guilty. What if he was worried about her? She shrugged. She didn't want to talk to him if he was going to do a number. She'd wait until she got back and then face the music. And think about what was really going on with her and Josh another day. A confrontation wasn't going to be fun. Why ruin a good mood and such a beautiful day?

Lily hustled back into the apartment at four o'clock, calling out to Sam as she did. After she took him for a long walk around the block, she fed him, gave him a fresh bowl of water, hung up her coat, and spread out her purchases. First there were the long cream-colored flax curtains she'd bought for her bedroom at one of the discount bed and bathroom stores on Sixth Avenue. She'd hang them tomorrow morning. Next was the Indian-print tablecloth she'd gotten at ABC Carpet that she would use to cover the large round glass table that she'd bought from one of her coworkers. She planned to use the table in her dining area and figured the cloth would warm up the space. Besides, she liked the colors that were in the cloth and planned to use them throughout the apartment. The yellows and oranges would brighten up the room and be a nice contrast to the cream-colored walls. Now, if she could find a neutral-colored couch, she decided, she could pull the whole thing together with throw pillows and plants and maybe even find a print or two for the walls. But she should probably wait on the couch since she'd gone a bit over budget on her dress.

She'd found the dress in a little shop in the Village. Although she'd looked throughout the day, even trying some of the funky clothes in ABC Carpet, it was after lunch that she'd gone down to the Village and spotted the dress in the window of the tiny store. It was pale gray, long and filmy, and unlike anything she'd ever owned.

She wasn't even going to try it on but once she poked her head into the store and asked about the dress, the saleslady insisted, promising her that she'd be very surprised when she did. As soon as Lily slipped it on, she felt like a princess—a sexy but demure princess. As she looked in the mirror in the dressing room she could not keep herself from twirling around in a circle, liking the feel of the fabric and the way it slid down her long thin frame. But when she saw the price tag she cringed. It was more than she was used to spending. Then she looked back at her reflection. Wonderful—as good as anything she'd ever worn. Would she be able to wear it again? Of course, all her friends were getting married. She'd have plenty of opportunities. Besides, probably no one at Maria's wedding would be at any of the others. Would Josh like it? Good question. She didn't have a clue. He had very definite ideas about what looked good on her and this filmy, sexy dress may not be among them. She shrugged. She loved it and wasn't about to let it go. She hadn't felt this pretty in a long time—maybe forever.

Remembering her struggle, Lily took the dress out of its wrappings and held it up against herself and looked in the mirror. She had been right to buy it, she decided, observing her reflection. It was beautiful and she knew she would enjoy wearing it.

The phone suddenly rang, jarring her out of her thoughts. Her stomach jolted when she glanced at her watch. She knew exactly who would be calling. After carefully hanging the dress up on the back of her closet door she went over to answer the phone.

"Lily," he said. "I've been frantic. Are you okay?"

She took a deep breath before answering, steeling herself for the inevitable. She intended to be honest— or reasonably so. Anything else would be immature; he might be her future husband. They needed to deal with each other as equal partners. "I just got in from shopping," she said. "I spent the day in New York."

"I haven't been able to reach you since Thursday. That's two days!"

"I'm fine," she said. She knew he'd start with a guilt trip. She supposed she should be flattered that he'd been worried, but his concern felt more like an albatross around her neck than anything comforting.

"What'd you do last night?" he continued. "I kept calling but you weren't there."

She sighed. "I was here, but I was really tired so I took the phone off the hook."

"You what?" he sputtered.

She squeezed her eyes and took a deep breath. Then she sat down. This was going to be more difficult than she'd thought. "I had a tough day in court and just wanted to be alone. I didn't think you'd call until after I was asleep and I was really tired."

There was a long pause before Josh said anything. "What if there'd been an emergency?"

She didn't answer right away. "Was there?"

"No, but there could have been."

She didn't respond.

He sighed. "I was worried," he finally said, the tone of his voice not as strident. He really did sound as if he had been concerned. "I haven't spoken to you since Thursday night and I wondered where you were and if anything was wrong."

Neither of them said anything for a moment.

"I'm glad you're okay," he finally said. "I was worried."

She heard him sigh.

"So where did you go in the City?" he asked eventually.

She told him about her day, the drapes, the tablecloth, and then the dress that she bought.

"Maria's just announced that she's getting married in a few weeks," she explained. "When I saw this dress I figured it would be perfect. Besides," she added defensively, "there will be a lot of other weddings I can wear it to."

"So when is this wedding?" Josh asked.

Lily told him the date, suddenly realizing that he probably expected that he would be going with her. He was, after all, her boyfriend. That it hadn't even crossed her mind set off alarms that she was loath to answer, though she knew she was going to have to sooner or later. This relationship was not doing well. There was no denying it as much as she would like to.

"Honey, I can't get out that soon. Last time I came I used up all my favors getting people to cover for me. It's going to have to be a few months before I can get all the way to the East Coast. It's one reason why picking a place halfway makes sense. Then I won't have to take as much time off. In fact," he said, his voice suddenly lower, his words more spaced apart, "I was thinking that we should plan a trip soon. It's not good for us to be separated for such long periods of time."

Lily didn't answer right away. Too many feelings were colliding inside her head. "I understand," she said. "I figured you probably couldn't come. But I've got to go to the wedding," she said. "It's a big deal for Maria and she's a new friend. I want to be there for her. And you're right," she added. "We could meet somewhere in between. It's not good for us to be this far apart for so long."

"One of the reasons I was trying to call you," he said, "was that they're giving me my own caseload here. They need the help and think I can do it."

"That's great," she said. From what he had told her, she knew that it was a real feather in his cap. It was unusual for someone as new as him to have that much responsibility. "You must feel really good about that."

"I do, but it's going to mean a lot more work."

"Is it going to affect our getting together?"

"Well, that's the thing. My time will actually be more my own, so if we schedule it right I should be able to get at least two days off at a time. I'll just have to work harder when I get back."

"Sounds good," she said, "and anyway, your success there should help wherever you go."

"That's what I figure. Any sacrifices we have to make here we'll get back. This promotion, and that's really what it is, is going to look good on my résumé."

She hung up shortly afterward continuing to feel confused and conflicted. Josh had been much more conciliatory than she'd ever expected him to be even if the conversation inevitably came back to him. And of course he wanted to share his good news. She felt guilty that she hadn't called him after she turned the phone back on. And maybe he was changing and becoming more sensitive to her needs, though perhaps that was wishful thinking. He still wasn't terribly interested in what went on in her life and he still did put his career first. He probably always would. Was she willing to put up with that: Josh calling the shots and putting himself first? Had it always been like that with him? She didn't know. She wanted to think they had both changed. Otherwise, it didn't make sense. The question now was, where was this relationship going? She would have to think about that one. But she should go out to see him. And soon. Unfortunately, the thought of going out there didn't fill her with the excited anticipation that it used to. Instead, she saw the trip as something that she should do, not wanted to do, like visiting her mother.

As for his not being able to go to Maria's wedding, she was struck by how alarmed she was that he might go. It meant she didn't have to deal with the fact that she'd already planned to go with Michael. She had to wonder if Michael and she were just friends, how come she was more excited about going with him to the wedding? She was even excited about having dinner with him and his family the next day. She went to bed that night with an engrossing novel. There were too many confusing things going on in her life and she wasn't ready to face them.

Chapter Thirteen

Lily knew she was putting too much thought into what she would wear to Michael's mother's house for dinner. First she'd pulled out her long denim skirt, black leather boots, and a black turtleneck, then changed into jeans, afraid she was going to be too dressed up, and finally back to a short navy corduroy skirt and red wool sweater. Maybe Michael's mother took Sunday dinner seriously. Lily wanted to be sure she was dressed appropriately. She wasn't sure what she was getting into or even why this lady wanted to meet her. Michael came by in his Jeep at about three o'clock and when she opened the door to greet him, she figured from the look on his face that she must have guessed right about what to wear.

"The apartment is only a few blocks away," he said, putting Sam's leash on his collar. "Want to walk or would you rather we ride?"

"Walking sounds good," she said. "I hadn't realized you all lived that close."

"Yeah," he said, "I only grew up a few blocks from here. My mother did too. No one in the family has ever strayed too far."

They walked across the park and to the other side. Lily had to increase her pace to keep up with Michael's long strides. As they walked, Michael pointed out landmarks from his childhood and buildings that he coveted. The neighborhood gradually changed from brownstones and low buildings to a mix of small apartment buildings. Suddenly he turned into a four-story brick building about ten blocks from her apartment. There was a low, black iron gate enclosing the small square of grass in front of the house and manicured bushes growing on either side of the front door. Lily followed Michael's lead and carefully wiped her feet on the welcome mat at the front door.

"My mother lives on the first floor," he explained as he led her down the hall to the back of the building, "so she gets the garden. My uncle lives on the second," he said, gesturing toward the stairs. "My brothers share the third floor and I've got the top, which means I also have access to the roof."

Lily nodded. It sounded nice if you really liked your family. She couldn't imagine living that close to hers. It wasn't that she didn't love them, but she was sure that rubbing shoulders with them on a daily basis would never work. Her brothers were so much older that she hardly knew them and she suspected that they still thought they could boss her around as their little sister.

She knew from experience that her mother had so many opinions—most of which Lily disagreed with, including her take on Josh—that they would constantly clash.

Michael knocked on the apartment door and Pat opened it to greet them. "Ma," he called as he let them inside.

Meanwhile, Sam, who'd been busy sniffing at everything in his path, had gone wild with excitement at the sight of Pat and was circling around him. Lily quickly scanned the living room to make sure there were no breakables in Sam's path. Pat, instead of trying to settle Sam down, was laughing and encouraging him and making matters worse. It was in the middle of this chaos that Michael's mother walked into the room.

From what her sons had told her, Lily was not surprised that Mrs. Frascato was small in stature, around five feet tall. But unlike the stereotypical Italian mother who was gray-haired and rotund, Michael's mother looked more like her son Pat. She was slim, fashionably dressed, and wore her blond-streaked hair short. Lily was glad she'd put some thought into what she had worn, noting Michael's mother's beautifully tailored slacks, slim-fitting gray wool sweater, and her carefully applied makeup.

"Welcome," said Mrs. Frascato, extending her hand. "I've heard so much about you and Sam from my boys that I had to meet you both."

Lily returned her greeting, nodding in response. "I've heard about you too," she said, "and it's very kind of you to have us for dinner. I only hope that Sam behaves himself. I haven't had him that long so I don't know how he'll act, or what I'll do if he misbehaves."

Mrs. Frascato shook her head. "Not to worry. One of the boys can deal with him." She glanced into the next room where Sam was already stretched out between Pat and Anthony in front of the Giants game on television. "I really don't think it's going to be a problem." She shook her head, continuing to look over at them. "Though it does make me think that maybe I should have given in and gotten them a dog when they were growing up."

Michael had left the room with their coats. "Get Lily some wine while I take her into the kitchen and show her some of your handiwork," she said to Michael when he returned from hanging up their coats.

Michael looked amused at his mother's bossiness, and went to fetch the wine.

The kitchen was a large square room at the back of the house overlooking a small garden filled with fading flowers, herbs, and vegetables. Lily recognized some withering zucchini and tomato plants and spotted some squash still on vines. A wrought-iron table and chairs were on the small brick patio in the middle of the garden. There was also a small tree, the leaves of which were still turning. Lily imagined that the spot was quite lovely in the summer when the flowers were in bloom and the tree was full of leaves and provided shade.

"This kitchen was Michael's first foray into design and construction," said Mrs. Frascato. She pointed to the butcher-block countertops and open shelves that filled one wall of the room. "He bought the building and then learned on the job. When we first moved in here this room was dark and dreary and there wasn't enough storage space. He was working construction that summer and would come home at night and talk about what kinds of homes he'd seen. I think about halfway through the summer it dawned on him that he could apply a lot of what he learned on the job right here in this house. Before I knew it, he was working into the night reconfiguring the space. He started with those shelves, and it wasn't long after that that he was knocking down walls and putting in windows." She beamed proudly. "It was pretty amazing."

Lily looked around the room with interest. Although it wasn't high-tech and trendy, it was everything a kitchen ought to be: warm, cozy, and filled with light. She was also conscious of the wonderful cooking smells that filled the room. Mrs. Frascato took the lid from a large pot on the stove and stirred the red sauce that was simmering. Then she opened the oven door and checked on what looked to be eggplant parmesan. "I hope you like Italian food," she said. "It's my sons' favorite, so that's what I always make on Sunday when they come for dinner."

Lily nodded and grinned. "Of course I do. What's not to like?"

Mrs. Frascato returned Lily's smile and then looked around the room as if to see if there was anything else to be done. "The eggplant just needs a few more minutes so let's go into the living room away from the television so we can hear ourselves think. You can tell me about yourself and how you like living in Jersey City. I understand you're not from around here."

As they sipped their wine Lily began to tell Mrs. Frascato how it was that she came to New Jersey after law school. She wasn't three sentences into her tale when Michael called out from the other room. "Now don't go interrogating her, Ma. She's a lawyer, originally from Baltimore, who is renting one of our apartments and happens to have a dog that your sons are crazy about. That's all you need to know."

Mrs. Frascato looked over at Lily and grinned. "He thinks I'm a gossip. I'm really not," she said. "I'm just interested in my boys and their friends."

Lily returned her grin and nodded. "I know," she said, meaning it. "I'm the same way. And I didn't feel as if you were prying. If we don't have time today and you're really interested, I'll give you the whole saga the next time we meet."

They didn't have any more time then since dinner was ready, and after Mrs. Frascato put the food on the table and called her sons in, there was hardly a chance to get a word in edgewise. But Lily had a good time. She enjoyed hearing Pat's tales from the firehouse and wondered at his energy to do any work on the apartment. Anthony was not as chatty about his job, but he did fill them in on what was going on down at city hall since his new girl-friend worked there. Michael talked about the courtroom and some of the crazy antics that went on there, drawing Lily into the conversation. Before she knew it she was telling her own stories and putting her two cents in when advice was asked for. Mrs. Frascato was up and down, constantly serving platters of food and refilling glasses from a pitcher of homemade wine, peppering each of them with questions and observations. Lily got up once to help her with a platter, but Mrs. Frascato told her to sit down. "You're a guest here," she said, "and in my house, guests don't wait on us. Don't worry about me. Traditionally my sons do the dishes and while they do, you and I can sit in the living room and maybe even finish our conversation."

After dinner, just as she said, Lily and Mrs. Frascato did go and sit while the brothers did the dishes. However, they never did get to finish their conversation because Michael kept interrupting them, calling out questions for his mother or comments to Lily from the kitchen. Nevertheless, it was a great evening. When Lily looked at her watch and saw it was past nine she couldn't believe her eyes. The time had flown by and she feared she was in danger of outstaying her welcome. Quickly she got up from the couch in the living room where they'd gone to sit after dinner and explained that she had to go.

"We enjoyed having you," said Mrs. Frascato. "It's nice to have another woman in the house. My sons have had girlfriends, but for some reason they don't invite them over for dinner." She winked. "I suspect they're afraid of what I'll say to them."

Michael got Lily's coat and the leash and came back with a container of leftovers. "Eggplant," he said grinning. "You must have made a good impression. Ma usually only sends home leftovers with family."

After turning back to thank Mrs. Frascato for dinner they were on their way.

"She's great," said Lily.

Michael nodded. "Has strong opinions on practically everything, but she is great. I'm very lucky."

They walked a ways in silence and then Michael spoke. "She's right about us not bringing anyone home. We think she'd intimidate most of the girls we know, particularly when she starts asking questions."

"I don't think she means anything by it," said Lily.

"That may be," said Michael, "but not everyone understands that." He paused. "I knew you wouldn't be intimidated, but then again you're different."

"I'm different?"

"Yeah. You're already your own person. I've watched you enough in court to know you're not going to be put off by someone like her." He paused. "Besides," he added, glancing at her sideways, "you're not looking to snare me."

There was an awkward silence. Lily figured she had to say something to break it. "And other people are?"

He gave a nervous laugh. "Yeah. To the locals around here I'm a big deal. I own a couple of buildings and I've got benefits . . ." His voice trailed off.

"So, is there someone special?" She found herself holding her breath, waiting for the answer, puzzled that his answer was important to her.

"No," he said. "I've dated a lot, but no one special. Not that I would mind, but there isn't."

"And your brothers?" For some reason now that she'd brought it up, Lily was anxious to get off the subject of Michael and his girlfriends, or lack thereof.

"Pat's got his eye on someone he knew from school and I wouldn't be surprised if something comes of it. She's a nice girl. As for Anthony, as you now know, he's seeing Cindy, the woman who works down at city hall. I'm not sure how serious they are, but listening to him tonight, it sounds as if he likes her quite a bit."

They'd reached her building. Michael walked her up to the front door and waited while she and Sam went inside. "Thanks a lot," said Lily. "I had a really nice time." And she meant it. That was as nice a Sunday as she'd spent in a long time.

She closed the door and was about to turn off the lights in the living room when there was a knock. She looked through the peep hole. It was Michael. "About next Saturday," he said when she opened the door. "How about if I come down here with my Jeep and park it here so we can take your car?"

"I could come and get you," she said.

Michael shook his head. "Absolutely not. I'll come by for you. You'll be all dressed up. Besides, my mother knows you now and would have my head if she saw you picking me up."

She grinned. "Okay. I'm convinced." She paused. "You've got a nice family," she said. "I had a really nice time."

He looked down at her and smiled and then suddenly leaned over and kissed her on the cheek.

He was down the steps before she could react. "See you next week," he called over his shoulder. "Sleep tight."

She shut the door and leaned her head against it.

What was that all about? A brotherly kiss, right? She didn't have any other kind of feelings for him, did she? If that was the case, why was she suddenly grinning? She usually had a pretty good radar about men, at least she had always thought she did, but with Michael she was very confused. At the very least his signals were mixed. But she was beginning to think that he really did find her attractive and that maybe he didn't see her like a sister. Maybe he was interested in her. She puttered around the kitchen, scooping coffee into the filter for tomorrow's brew, getting fresh water for Sam. If that was the case, why only a peck, why not a full head-on kiss? "Ladies' man!" she muttered, remembering Tracy's remarks. "Not when it comes to me!" She looked down at the dog. "Not a single move, unless you count that peck on the cheek." She sighed. "I guess I should be relieved, right?" She shook her head. "How come I'm not?"

Chapter Fourteen

Maria took the following week off from work to get ready for her wedding. All the cases that would have been heard in court that week were adjourned until after she came back. Because there were no scheduled court hearings, Lily had a chance to catch up on her paperwork in the office. She got so much accomplished by Wednesday that she felt comfortable enough to take the day off and look for furniture for her apartment. She thought she would try IKEA, which was only a few miles away, just past Newark airport, in Elizabeth. Friends from work had told her that besides having good prices, the store had a great selection of well-designed furniture. After she checked to see how much room she had left on her credit card, she took a few measurements of the rooms in the apartment, including the living room and the kitchen, and headed off with high hopes.

Three hours later she was in IKEA's parking lot

with a cartload of boxes, including a couch, coffee table, glasses and dishes, trying to figure out how she was going to fit it all into her car. After stuffing every crevice of her compact and, with the help of the IKEA crew, tying the couch to the roof, she slowly made her way back to Jersey City. As she pulled into a space close to her building, she puzzled over how she was going to manage the next step of getting it all into her apartment. Her prayers were answered when she spotted Pat walking out the front door of her building. When he saw her and her carload, he shook his head, laughed, and came over.

"Looks like you had a day for yourself," he said.

She nodded. "I'm glad to run into you."

"You're even luckier than that," he said, motioning toward her building where both Anthony and Michael were just coming down the steps. They headed over too.

Lily suddenly felt a little off balance. She wasn't surprised to see Anthony and Pat but she hadn't been expecting to see Michael, figuring he'd be in court. Seeing him unexpectedly like this brought her up short and gave her pause. She was afraid to think why. It couldn't be because he was wearing nicely fitting jeans and a worn flannel shirt—both more flattering that his courthouse uniform. She wasn't that kind of girl.

"You took the day off too?" he asked.

She nodded as she smiled up at him. She'd always noticed that he had intense eyes, but why was she suddenly finding them unnerving, or more precisely, why did her heart beat faster when he looked in her direction? She mentally shrugged off her reaction and tried to focus on the fact that these three big powerful men who were her friends were going to help her get all this stuff into her apartment.

Sam greeted them at the door with great excitement, obviously delighted to have all the people he loved in one room together. Lily tried to calm him down and keep him from jumping as the three men carried the furniture into the apartment. He was getting in their way and she was afraid he'd trip one of them or cause them to drop one of the boxes. In desperation she put on his leash and took him for a quick walk while they carried everything in.

It hadn't taken long for the three men to empty her car and by the time she got back from walking Sam they'd gotten everything into the house. Michael was standing in the middle of the living room, surveying her purchases. "Unless you have a reason for waiting," he said, "we might as well unpack this stuff and set it up. If it's like most of what they sell," he added, gesturing toward the still-unopened boxes that contained the coffee table and dishes and glassware, "the table is probably going to come in several pieces so we better get started."

Lily threw up her hands. "You sure you wouldn't mind? I'm going to owe you guys big time!"

Michael grinned. "You don't owe us anything. We've got it down to a science. Ma is one of their biggest customers."

Pat looked up from the pile of wood that presumably would turn into a table and smiled. "But I do have one question."

She looked over expectantly.

"Got any beer?"

"Sure," she said and smiled as she headed for the fridge. She still had most of the six-pack from when Arlene and her boyfriend had come by to see the apartment. She pulled out four beers and grabbed a bottle opener and a box of pretzels she had in the back of her cabinet, and came back to the living room where she started to pop off the tops of the beers and pass them around, keeping one for herself. "Can I get you guys a pizza? Or I could cook up some pasta."

The three shook their heads. "This is perfect," said Pat, "and all I've got time for, especially after a long day. I've got a class in half an hour and I usually eat after that," said Pat.

"I've got my kids to coach," said Michael, "and this guy over here," he said, pointing to Anthony, "has a hot date."

Anthony shook his head. "Don't listen to him. He's jealous. I'm just taking Cindy out for a burger."

While they drank their beers, the three brothers continued to work. Each of them had grabbed a box and was busy unpacking it. Besides the table, the only other thing that required teamwork was the couch. But even that didn't take them much time. After they were finished with the coffee table, they got a knife from the kitchen and got to work cutting the plastic and paper that were wrapped around the couch. When they were done, each grabbed a side of the couch and picked it up.

"Where do you want to put it?" asked Michael.

Before she could respond, Pat answered, "Obviously

in front of the television." The others nodded and placed it there after testing several positions until they were satisfied that the spot they chose had the best angle for viewing. When they were happy with where the couch was, they placed the coffee table directly in front of it after sitting on the couch and measuring the comfortable distance for snack and feet placement. Everyone, including Lily, approved.

She looked around. "I just need to get some plants, but that shouldn't be too difficult, and think about whether to paint."

Patrick looked at his watch. He turned to Anthony. "I've got to get going. How about running me over to school so I'm not late?"

The older brother nodded and then turned to Michael. "I assume you can manage the rest?"

Michael grinned. "We should be okay."

The two men hurried out the door while Lily and Michael stacked the new dishes and glassware on the counter to be washed. It was starting to feel awkward standing there with Michael when Sam came bounding over to them, having finished the can of food Lily had given him. "This guy probably wouldn't mind a real walk," she said, going back into the kitchen to get the leash.

"Why don't I come with you," said Michael. "It's a beautiful night."

Lily nodded and grinned at Michael's remark as she followed him out of the apartment. She wished that she didn't feel so bashful and awkward. She knew him the best, so why was it so much easier with his brothers? It wasn't because he was more attractive, as they were all good-looking. But it was Michael, not his brothers, that she was attracted to; she needed to admit that. She glanced over at him walking beside her. But that didn't mean anything, did it? It was okay to think someone was attractive without it meaning anything, right? So she needed to relax and enjoy these three new friends and stop worrying. She looked over again and smiled, hoping she looked more relaxed than she felt.

Michael smiled back. "So it looks like you're pretty well set."

Lily agreed. "As I said, I've got a few things to do like plants and stuff, which should be easy, but I'm pretty much finished except for figuring out some shelves for the bedroom."

"We can take care of that," he said.

"You've already done enough," she said.

"But why not? We're right here in the building and have the materials. It'll take no time at all."

She grinned. "When you put it like that . . . ," she said.

"Show me where you want the shelves," he said when they got back from walking Sam. "One of us can start on them tomorrow."

She nodded. She couldn't say no. She led him into her bedroom, hoping he couldn't tell how awkward she felt being alone with him. She squashed her discomfort and showed him the wall she was talking about. "If I put a couple of shelves here I won't need a table and it won't be so cluttered. I could keep my alarm clock, a lamp, and some books on it."

He came over to where she was standing next to her bed and motioned toward the wall. "How high do you want the shelves to go?"

She leaned closer to show him, so close she could smell the clean simple smell of his soap and shampoo, faintly mixed with what she could only imagine to be the essence of him. When she raised her hand to show him the height of the shelves, their hands met. She froze, unable to move, only aware that the feel of his calloused fingers on hers caused a warm sensation to run through her, right down to her core. Just for a moment time seemed to freeze as they both stared at their joined hands. She looked over and met his glance. "Well," she said, clearing her throat, "I—I guess you get the idea."

He nodded and abruptly moved away to the other side of the room. "Sounds good," he said after clearing his throat. "I'll talk to the guys tomorrow about it and we'll figure out who's going to do it." He grabbed a pencil out of his pocket and, turning back to the wall, bent down to mark off where the shelves would go.

Suddenly the phone rang. Michael's eyes focused on hers for a moment before he quickly stood up. "Let me get out of your hair," he said quickly. "I'm sure you've got things to do." He quickly strode out into the living room and headed for the door.

"Thanks for everything you've done," she said, following him out. "I don't know how I would have managed."

The phone continued to ring.

"Don't you want to get that?" Michael asked, gesturing toward the phone.

She shrugged and looked over at it as if she were just now aware of the ring. "I guess I'd better," she said.

"I'll let myself out," he said.

She reached down to answer the phone when Michael called out from the front door. "I'll pick you up at three, okay? The wedding starts at four and we don't want to be late."

"That's fine," she said, her hand now resting on the phone, which continued to ring.

Chapter Fifteen

The next day, back in her office in Newark, Lily got a call from Irene, the supervising caseworker. She sounded frightened. "I need to talk to you about the Romano family," she said, her voice higher than usual.

"Sure," said Lily. "What's up?"

"It would be easier to tell you in person," said Irene. "Are you coming to our office?"

Irene was not an alarmist. Something had to be wrong. "Of course," said Lily. "I'll be there in an hour." In the middle of the day, Lily figured she could easily get from Newark to Paterson within that time.

Lily quickly pulled the Romano file and reviewed her notes from the last hearing, when Judge Keegan had ordered Mr. Romano into anger management and told him he would not be back in his own house until he got a favorable report. At the time both Lily and Irene had been concerned that in spite of the court order, which included a restraining order, Mrs. Romano would not stand up to her husband. She saw him as the one with all the power in their family. And to a certain extent she was right. He controlled the money. Although he was supposed to be paying support payments, even when he wasn't living with her, Lily knew he was slow to do so. Shortly after that time in court she'd heard from Irene that Romano had been arrested when he violated the restraining order. He went back home and had gone after Mrs. Romano with a baseball bat. But this time, apparently empowered by the restraining order, Mrs. Romano had called the cops and her husband was arrested.

As soon as she got to the Paterson office Irene grabbed her. "Can we talk now?" Lily nodded and hustled her into a nearby conference room and shut the door.

"Sit down," Lily said, indicating the chair across from her at the conference table. "Tell me what's going on." She was concerned. This compact, middle-aged woman never got flustered about anything, including threats. What was it about this case that had her so stirred up?

"It's Mr. Romano," said Irene, leaning forward on the chair, her hands pressed against her thighs. "He has been calling me."

"Calling you? I thought he was in jail."

Irene shook her head. "They released him."

"What does he want from you? He should know it's not up to you to decide when he can go home."

Irene shook her head impatiently. "He says it's my fault that he was in jail and can't go back to his wife." She wrung her hands as she spoke.

"What about the restraining order that his wife filed?"

Irene shook her head. "You know how he is. He doesn't get it. Says that's his home—the only place he's got to live—at least that's what he's telling me. He says it's my fault that he's homeless and living on the streets."

"What did you tell him?"

"I told him he'd still be living at home if he kept his hands to himself. I told him I would set him up in counseling so he could resolve his issues and eventually go back to his wife."

"And he said?" Lily looked over at Irene questioningly.

"That I could kiss his butt."

"So he wasn't receptive," said Lily dryly. She'd been taking notes while Irene talked, but now looked up at her friend and colleague.

"Of course not! Not Mr. Romano. If he was receptive, he wouldn't be in this fix." She took a gulp of air and then continued with her story. "He started cursing at me, screaming over the phone." She shook her head and sighed, obviously recalling the incident. Then she put her shoulders back, leaned back in the chair and looked up at Lily. "But I could have dealt with that. Lots of abusive men do that. We see them every day. What's got me scared is that he told me he's going to make me sorry and that he could do that because he knows where I live. Isn't there something the law can do to protect me?"

Lily finally understood why Irene was so upset. This

case was different because Romano was prepared to go after Irene. "But do you think he really knows where you live?" she asked, hoping it wasn't true.

"I know he does!" said Irene. "He not only knows exactly where I live, he even has my home phone number."

"How did he get that?"

Irene shook her head. "I don't know. What I do know is that he's got it because he called me there."

Lily put her pen down and looked up. "You've got to file an order of protection."

"Will that work? He's not going to pay any attention."

"It's a start. And at least this way you can drag him into court. The judge is not going to look kindly at someone who's had a history of domestic violence, is out on bail, and is now threatening state employees. Don't forget, he's got a record now. The judge may lock him up just because he's threatening you."

"Do you think?"

Lily shook her head. "I can't promise you that the judge will do it, but it's what we have to work with and we certainly can try. And for starters you need to get over to family court this afternoon—the sooner, the better. You know how they hate to be kept late on Friday afternoons." She looked directly at Irene. "You said he says he's living in the streets. Is that really the case?"

Irene shook her head and made a face. "He says that, but in reality he's staying at his mother's."

"Good, because they'll want to serve him and we can use that address."

Irene nodded, looking relieved. At least it was something.

"After that, if he threatens you, you let him know that you filed and what that means."

"He won't care."

"He will if he goes to your house and you call the police. Don't forget, if that happens, they arrest him."

Irene nodded, finally looking more like herself. "I'll go over to court right now."

She got up and was about to leave Lily's office when something else occurred to Lily.

"Irene?"

She turned and looked at Lily.

"Are you living alone with the kids?" Irene had a boy and a girl, about ten and twelve.

Irene nodded.

"Isn't there someone you and the kids could stay with until this blows over? Maybe a close friend or a boyfriend?"

Irene shook her head. "We just moved into Paterson pretty recently and, as you know, my family is all in the Dominican Republic."

Lily didn't say anything for a minute. She didn't like the fact that Romano knew where Irene lived, but she wasn't sure how much more they could do until they had more against Mr. Romano. Right now what they had were threats. Threats would get them an order of protection, but not a restraining order since Irene didn't live with Romano and wasn't in a relationship with him. Was an order of protection enough with someone like Romano? Lily didn't think so. There had to be more.

But the trouble was that even if they got the police to patrol the house, they wouldn't be there twenty-four-seven. The resources of the Paterson Police Department were limited and they were not receptive to being asked to patrol a home unless they were sure the threat was real. Lily and Irene knew Romano was capable of violence, but would they be believed? Irene would have to go to court and find out.

She looked up at Irene and tried to be upbeat. "Tell the kids to be careful, okay?"

Irene frowned and then nodded. "I will, believe me."

Lily was still in the DYFS office when Gloria, the litigation specialist, approached. Her job was to write the complaints that they filed in court. If the office thought something should be in court, they would first discuss it with Lily before writing the complaint.

"I'm so glad you're here," said Gloria. "We have a situation."

Lily's heart sank. "Situation" was shorthand in their office for a serious problem that usually required court intervention. If Lily gave the okay after listening to the facts, the DYFS would go out and take the children into custody.

"So what's the problem?" said Lily, motioning for Gloria to sit down across from her.

"It's one of Aggie's cases," said Gloria, mentioning one of the supervisors in the office.

"Call her in," said Lily, "and let's figure this out."

Aggie came in and got right to the point. "We've got two cases," she said. "First one, caseworker goes out to the home because the school called us to report the kids are absent a lot. Five kids," she added. "Mom is on her own and the school is concerned because she seems overwhelmed."

"Overwhelmed" usually meant dirty house and dirty kids, neither of which warranted court intervention. But sometimes it meant that the kids were not getting enough to eat or that there was a boyfriend in the home who was threatening the kids. It was the caseworker's job to figure out the difference. Lily's job was to decide if it was serious enough to go to court.

Aggie continued. "We agreed with the school that the mother needed our help so we sent a caseworker out to check up on her and give her whatever support we thought she needed. Mother is young," she added, "about twenty-eight."

Lily didn't have to do the math to figure this lady must have started having these babies at about fourteen, which meant she didn't have much of an education or job experience. She probably needed financial assistance and would have a tough time keeping it all together.

"Okay," said Lily, "so we've got a young, overwhelmed mother—anything else?"

The supervisor nodded. "When the caseworker went out today, she found a child home alone."

Lily's heart sank. These were always the tough ones. What they had here was a single mother, overwhelmed, with no resources and no family, trying to hold on. They didn't want to penalize her if she was trying, but at the same time they couldn't leave the kids there if they were at risk.

"So tell me exactly what happened," said Lily when Amy, the caseworker for the family, came into Lily's office to provide the details.

Amy, who was not very old herself, leaned forward and began her story. "When I knocked on the door the child was reluctant to let me in, which . . . ," she said, looking around at the other women in the room, including her supervisor, "was not a bad thing. I asked him if his mother was there. He said no, explaining that she was taking his brothers to school. Then I asked him how old he was."

"And he said?" prompted Lily.

"Twelve."

Lily looked at her questioningly. "So what's the problem?"

Amy shook her head. "This is Ahmed that I was talking to and Ahmed is"—Amy paused and looked down at the case record in front of her—"four. He was four last month."

Lily grinned. It sounded like the little guy had guts. "So what did you say to Ahmed when he told you that?"

"I asked him if he was okay. He said he was fine and that he was watching television and if he could go back to it. I said he could, but to come and check with me at the next commercial. He agreed. I waited about ten minutes; Ahmed checked in twice and then the mother came home."

"Are they both here now?" asked Lily.

"Yes," said Amy. "They're in the small conference room waiting for us to decide what to do."

"How does the mother seem to you? Do you have any concerns about her?" asked Lily.

"Not really. She seems fine, just young with too much on her plate." She shrugged. "Who wouldn't be? But the boy is well taken care of and he knew not to let me in."

Lily didn't say anything for a minute. She hated taking kids from their parents when there was no real risk, even if there was enough to file. In those cases she looked for the loophole that would enable them to keep the child at home.

"I assume you've read her the riot act," said Lily. "You've told her she could be arrested for leaving a child that age home alone. You told her about all the kids who have died from fires that started when their mom ran down the street for groceries."

Amy nodded. "I did."

In the ensuing silence, Amy looked from Lily to Aggie and back to Lily, her eyebrows furrowed. "Are you suggesting we don't remove?"

Lily looked over at Aggie, Amy's supervisor. "What do you think?"

Aggie nodded. "If you think we can avoid it. We really don't want to remove Ahmed if we don't have to. Except for being left home alone, we have no concerns. There was food in the house. He was clean and so was the apartment. We just wanted to make sure.

She turned to Amy. "Make sure that the mother understands the danger she put Ahmed in," she said.

Amy nodded and left the room to go and tell Ahmed's mother the good news. Aggie stayed behind. "I'm glad you came up with that solution. I really didn't want to take the child. It's always so traumatic for the little ones." She paused and sighed heavily before continuing, "We've got another case," she said. "Unfortunately more serious, I think."

"Shoot," said Lily, settling back in her chair to listen.

"Vicky's the caseworker on this one," said Aggie. "I'll call her in now."

Moments later Vicky, a middle-aged woman of Colombian descent came in. She'd been a caseworker for over twenty-five years and was very good at her job. "You're not going to like this one," she said when she took a seat. "I don't know what to do with Ms. Muniz," she continued in heavily accented English. She was bilingual and went out on many of the Hispanic cases. "I could see she was overwhelmed," Vicky continued. "Like most of our clients, she's a young mother, all alone with four little girls. She's got no education, no job experience, so of course she's got to be overwhelmed." Vicky paused and looked around the room to make sure they were all listening.

Lily certainly was listening and waiting for the other shoe to drop. Would it be removal, supervision, or could they give some assistance so the kids could stay in the home? These were decisions that had to be made so that kids would be safe and they all could sleep at night, knowing they'd done the right thing and none of the children on their watch were at risk.

Vicky went on. "I sent her to Job Corps," she said,

referring to the program in New Jersey that provided training for the unskilled. "I gave her an application for low-income housing, food stamps, and Christmas presents last December. But I knew that someday we'd reach this point. She's always so distracted."

Vicky sighed. "But today was much worse than just being distracted."

Lily waited.

"I happened to be driving by their house today, not even going there, when I looked up, and what did I see?" She looked around the room again as if to make sure she had their attention. "The three girls were on the roof of the building. On a six-story rooftop! They were playing up there! No railing, no barriers, one of those girls could have fallen off and been killed." She paused and shook her head. "Of course, I pulled over and went right up."

"Where was Ms. Muniz?" asked Lily.

Vicky shook her head. "You'd wonder," she said. She wrung her hands and took a deep breath before continuing. "We still don't know. She wasn't home and the girls didn't know where she was."

"Did they tell you why they weren't in school?"

"Teachers' conferences, they had a half day. Luckily the little one was at day care, or she would have been up there too. She does everything the big ones do, if she can."

"Did you bring them all in here?"

Vicky nodded. "What choice did I have? They are all here except the little one. Someone's got to pick her up now." She shook her head. "Such a foolish woman.

Those girls could have been dead right now if I hadn't driven by."

"So we'll have to go to court on this one," said Lily. Both Vicky and Aggie nodded. There wasn't any question on a case like this. Those girls had been at real risk. Even so, Lily quickly went through the legal analysis. The state of New Jersey could only remove children if there was imminent risk of danger to them. It was clear in this case that they had risk. If Vicky hadn't picked up those kids one of them could have fallen off the roof and been killed. Now they would have to find the mother and petition the court for custody. Lily had no doubt that the court would grant it under the circumstances, but it was going to be some scene.

Because it was late Friday afternoon with an hour before the courts closed, they had until Monday at noon to file.

"Is someone in the office who can write the complaint?" asked Lily.

"Tamika's not too busy," said Aggie, referring to one of the paralegals.

"Good." Luckily, Tamika churned out a nice document. "Have her do a draft before she leaves tonight and e-mail it to me at my office. We want to be ready first thing Monday morning."

Lily looked at her watch. It was four thirty. She needed to go back to her office and wait for Tamika's draft so they could be ready to file on Monday morning.

By six o'clock she had e-mailed the corrections to Tamika and was ready to head out. If there wasn't any traffic she'd just make her six forty-five nail appointment and only have her hair to deal with tomorrow. She loved her new dress and was looking forward to getting all gussied up for Maria's wedding.

Her cell phone rang just as she was about to leave. It was Josh.

"Thought I'd catch you before I started tonight's rotation," he said.

"I was just about to leave the office," said Lily. She didn't tell him she was getting her nails done, otherwise he'd probably figure it was a special occasion. Lily wasn't someone who got her nails done once a week. She didn't want him to realize that, for her, Maria's wedding was special. As much, she had to admit, because she was going with Michael as because it was Maria's wedding. Honestly, nails, hair, new dress? She obviously wanted to look good!

"So what are you up to this weekend?" asked Lily brightly.

"The usual," he said. "I'm on until six tomorrow morning. I'll sleep until noon. Maybe go jogging if it's nice, to the gym if it's not." He paused as if hesitating.

"Sounds good," said Lily, filling the silence between them. "What about tomorrow night? Are you working?"

Josh didn't answer right away. "Not really," he finally said. "I'm not sure what I'm going to do. Someone at the clinic is having a party. Maybe I'll go to that."

"That's good," said Lily, feeling less guilty by the minute. "You should get out and socialize. It's not good to stay in alone."

"You think?" asked Josh.

"Yeah," said Lily firmly. "I definitely think."

"We should meet soon," Josh said abruptly, "somewhere in the middle like Chicago or Cleveland."

"You're right," said Lily, trying to work up some enthusiasm, realizing that she wasn't looking forward to meeting up with him in the slightest. But she couldn't just end this, could she? After all these years, didn't she have a responsibility to figure out if her lack of interest was temporary, that her growing feelings for Michael were really only a crush? Of course they should meet, she told herself. Being separated like this was obviously terrible for their relationship. They hardly knew each other anymore and lately had trouble even coming up with things to talk about. Maybe it was simply too late for meetings, but shouldn't she try to find out?

"Why don't you look into getting a ticket? Check the prices for those two places. I'm off for the weekend at the end of the month. We could do it then," suggested Josh.

"Good idea," she said. "I'll take care of that Monday."

"I'll let you go," said Josh. "Have a good weekend."

Chapter Sixteen

Lily was putting the finishing touches on her makeup when the doorbell rang. She scrutinized herself in the mirror, shook her head several times, watching her newly shorn locks fall back into place, just the way the hairdresser had styled them, and smiled back at her reflection with satisfaction. The dress was just as perfect as she'd thought when she bought it and it showed off her willowy frame. The silver color was great with her dark brown hair, particularly when she was wearing crimson-colored lipstick, which is what she had on today. The color was also what she chose for her toenails, which were peeking out of her strappy sandals. They had been a last-minute purchase and fortunately had been a bargain. She took one last glance to make sure everything was in order and then, after turning out the bathroom light, hurried to answer the door.

Michael looked wonderful. There was no other way

to put it. He was wearing a dark blue suit, crisp white shirt, and a red patterned tie. The suit fit like a glove and emphasized his long, rangy build. He grinned when he saw her, and then skimmed his eyes over her with what appeared to be appreciation. Lily felt a tingling response in the depths of her tummy, which she did her best to ignore. She'd always found Michael attractive, as anyone with eyes would, but there was something about his reaction to her and her response that felt more than just friend/coworker status. She suspected she would find out tonight. Although they could say they were driving to the wedding together because they lived in the same neighborhood, there did appear to be a definite attraction between them. On the other hand, nothing had been said. She supposed it was possible that they wouldn't even hang out together when they got to the reception. There probably would be other sheriffs and court personnel going and he could hang out with them while she managed on her own. But from the look in his eye and her response, she doubted it.

Michael cleared his throat. "Ready?" he said, looking at his watch. "If we leave now we should just make it. I listened to the traffic report on the way over and they're saying the Turnpike is tied up so we better take 1–9."

Lily nodded. "I just have to get my wrap," she said self-consciously, walking across the living room to pick up the pashmina shawl from the couch and feeling Michael's eyes upon her as she did.

"Dog been walked?"

"Uh-huh, I just took him out."

Michael leaned down and gave Sam's head a rub. "Pat will be by in a couple of hours to take you out," he told him, "so behave yourself until then." He opened the apartment door and motioned for Lily to go ahead of him out the door. She hoped as she did that her new dress was flattering from behind.

The first few minutes in the car were awkward. *We're friends*, Lily sternly reminded herself. *We also have stuff to talk about.*

"Haven't seen you in a few days," said Michael. "Things slow at the office?"

Lily shook her head, relieved to have a subject to focus on. "Not quite. In fact we'll be giving you some business on Monday. We had a removal but Vicky didn't take the kids until after twelve so we've got until Monday at noon," she said, explaining about the Muniz kids playing on the roof of their apartment building.

"But that wasn't our only crisis on Friday," said Lily, almost glad to have something so serious to talk about. "Irene has been receiving threats."

"Threats?" said Michael, his eyebrows arching. "What do you mean by threats?"

"Remember Mr. Romano, the man who abused his wife and kids?"

She looked over to see if he remembered. When he didn't immediately respond, she continued explaining. "You called in two other sheriffs because you thought he might act out."

Michael nodded, not saying anything as he maneuvered the last turn onto Route 1–9. Once they were again sailing along the highway, headed towards Route 3 and Paterson, he spoke. "Wasn't he the guy we had to lock up because he beat his wife so badly she landed in St. Joe's Hospital?"

Lily nodded. "Yeah, that's the one."

"He's stalking Irene? That doesn't sound good. What's the story?"

She told him about the threats and the fact that he blamed Irene for his being homeless.

"Irene have kids?"

"Two, a boy and a girl, middle-school age."

"Husband or man in her life?"

"Nope."

"So what's she doing to protect herself?"

"I told her to file an order of protection."

He shook his head. "That's not going to do it. All it will do is give her rights if he comes after her."

For a few minutes neither spoke. Lily was starting to feel sick. Michael was verbalizing all the fears she had tried to put out of her mind because she didn't see a solution. Irene could be in real danger and there wasn't anything that Lily could do to protect her. Even worse, perhaps all she'd done was give Irene false courage making her think she was protected.

Michael let out a deep sigh.

"What are you thinking?" asked Lily.

Michael glanced over at her. "I'm thinking that there's got to be something I can do to make sure she's okay. Can't let a dangerous bully like Romano get away with terrorizing people."

"But what can you possibly do?" asked Lily.

Michael shrugged. "I'm not sure, but let me think about it. There's got to be something." He paused while he merged into Route 3. "He can't just get away with it."

The traffic on Route 3 was heavier and demanded Michael's full attention for the next few minutes, and when it eased up and conversation resumed, it was about Maria's wedding and who would be there. "I'm guessing I'll only know the few people I met at her house, including her parents and Joe, of course," said Lily. "I don't think she invited anyone else from work."

Michael shrugged. "She might have invited the investigator from her office," he said, "and possibly one of the sheriffs that she used to work with, and maybe Tracy."

They arrived at church only minutes before the ceremony was scheduled to begin and quickly went inside. An usher, whom Lily recognized from the party as one of the groom's brothers, approached and offered his arm. "Which side," he said, "bride or groom?"

"Bride," said Lily as he led her to a pew about halfway down on the left side of the center aisle. Michael followed behind, but when it came time to enter the pew, he bent down toward her. "Let me go in first so you're on the outside," he said.

She looked at him questioningly.

He grinned. "I've been to a lot of weddings with my mother. If you're on the aisle you'll get a better view of the bride as she comes down."

Lily nodded and smiled. "Thanks. Your mother trained you well."

The first strains of the wedding march began and

Lily's eyes instantly filled with tears—a phenomenon that occurred when she heard those first familiar chords at every wedding she attended. But this time it almost seemed justified for Maria looked stunning, radiating happiness as she approached on the arm of her beaming father.

Lily glanced up to the front of the church to the waiting groom, who was grinning from ear to ear. Spontaneously Lily reached over and squeezed Michael's hand.

"I love weddings when the people are right for each other," she said.

Michael cocked his head in surprise and Lily quickly dropped his hand feeling her face suddenly heat up with embarrassment.

Michael put his arm around her and pulled her toward him. "I wouldn't have pegged you as a romantic," he said, smiling as he looked down at her.

Lily resisted the urge to pull back although the electricity between them was hard to ignore.

"I'm full of surprises," she said softly, turning her attention to the ceremony that was just beginning.

Maria's parents wanted a nuptial mass for their only daughter and Maria didn't have the heart to refuse them. The mass lasted an hour and by the time Michael and Lily got to the reception it was close to six. "I've got to make a call," said Michael when they arrived. "Where shall I look for you?"

Lily scanned the entryway searching for a familiar face. There were none except for Maria and Joe's relatives that she'd met at Maria's the week before, but they were talking to people Lily didn't know, so she decided not to intrude. "I'll be in the bar," she said, pointing to a dark, wood-paneled room where most of the party seemed to be headed.

Michael nodded. "See you in a few."

She was sipping a glass of white wine and munching on a plate of olives and cheese when Michael found her. He was carrying a beer and accompanied by a couple Lily recognized from Maria's party but hadn't met.

"Maria's cousin, Carmen," said Michael, "and her husband, Victor."

Lily reached over and shook their hands and was about to say something when another couple, followed by a third, joined them. Everyone was talking at once and it didn't take long for Lily to get swept up in conversations. After a second glass of wine, she felt as if she'd known these people, cousins of Maria and their spouses, for years. Every now and then she'd glance over at Michael to see how he was doing and each time it was the same. He'd be talking, laughing, and smiling. The wine flowed, with waiters coming by to pick up empty glasses and provide full fresh ones. Fortunately, the food was also plentiful. Lily nibbled on spicy sausages, marinated shrimp, and exotic items that she couldn't identify but that tasted delicious. Several times Maria floated by, always surrounded, but Lily did have a chance to congratulate her and give her a hug.

Maria nodded in the direction of her cousins. "I knew I wouldn't have to worry about you two!" She turned to her husband. "Didn't I tell you they'd find their niche?"

Her new husband grinned in acknowledgment before taking Maria by the hand, urging her forward. "You know your mother is waiting for more pictures. Let's get them over with so we can really enjoy this party."

He turned to Lily. "Wait until you hear the band we've got. Everyone will be dancing."

Shortly after that they were called into the main dining room for dinner. There was no assigned seating but before Lily even had a chance to wonder where she and Michael would sit, Maria's cousins insisted that they join them. As they settled themselves in and waited to be served the first course of vegetable soup, it was finally calm enough for everyone to introduce themselves. The three women were Maria's first cousins. They and their husbands had all grown up together in the same neighborhood as Maria.

"The four of us were inseparable in high school and when we commuted to Jersey City for college," said Rachel.

"It wasn't until Maria went off to law school and the three of us started working that we weren't in lock step," explained Carmen. "We got married, she had her daughter, took the bar, and became a lawyer."

Angela's eyes twinkled. "Aunt Ida," she explained, "was fit to be tied."

Victor leaned over. "Aunt Ida invited the entire neighborhood to a party when Maria came home with Joe."

"He was the first Puerto Rican she had ever dated," explained Angela.

"And he married her," added Victor.

Lily was laughing. "And I thought I had pressure."

All eyes turned to look at her, including Michael's. "You?"

Lily laughed. "Of course," she said. "Why should I be any different?"

Victor shrugged. "You're an Anglo."

The others nodded, including Michael, who added, apparently for clarification, "He means WASP."

Lily grinned and shook her head, scanning the seven of them. "So? What do you think? WASP mothers don't worry about their daughters getting married?"

"It's not the same," protested Angela. "WASPs are cooler about it. They don't call up crying in the middle of the night."

"Or say novenas," offered Rachel.

The others nodded in recognition and agreement.

Lily smiled in response. "Maybe so, but they pressure nonetheless. They're just more subtle about it. Believe me," she added, "WASP mothers can be just as annoying."

Suddenly Michael's beeper went off. He stood up and nodded to Lily and the others. "If you'll excuse me," he said. "I've got a call I've got to take." He turned to Lily. "It shouldn't take long."

"That's okay," she said. "I'll be fine. Take whatever time you need."

While they'd been eating their first course the band had been softly playing guitar music. Suddenly the music got louder and Lily recognized a popular Latin song at the same time as half the room rose to their feet to dance, including everyone at her table.

"Come on," said Rachel, motioning for Lily to join them.

"That's okay," said Lily, "I can wait for Michael."

"You don't understand," said Angela. "You don't need a partner to dance here."

Lily looked at her doubtfully.

"Really," said Rachel. "Come on. You'll see."

Lily shrugged and got up and slowly followed them. But even as she trailed them across the floor to an open spot where the others were waiting, she already was feeling the rhythm of the music and was glad they'd insisted.

Angela motioned for her to join them in a circle and the five moved to the Latin beat. At first Lily felt shy and self-conscious. Although she recognized the song from the radio, she'd never been in a Latin club or danced to this kind of music. But whether it was because of the music or the congeniality of the crowd, the atmosphere was infectious and before she knew it she was moving to the song as if she'd been doing it her whole life. When she looked around at the others on the dance floor she saw that people of all ages were up and dancing and enjoying themselves. She couldn't remember the last time she'd had so much fun.

Michael appeared and slid in next to her and immediately picked up the beat. "Remind me to tell you something when we sit down," he said, leaning over to speak directly into her ear.

She nodded.

When the next song started their group continued dancing, but separated into couples and Lily was for the first time facing Michael. He reached over and drew her closer to him. "You look very pretty today," he said.

She could feel her face heat up with feelings that she couldn't quite identify. Nevertheless she didn't try to hide the pleasure his words gave her. He looked pretty good himself. He moved to the music with the grace of an athlete and was easy to follow. He'd obviously danced to this kind of music before and whenever Lily was unsure, she'd just look over and mimic his motion.

Lily caught sight of Maria at the other end of the dance floor. Michael followed her gaze.

"She looks pretty busy right now," he said, pointing to the ring bearer and flower girl dancing with Maria. "But she said she'd be by our table later."

Lily nodded. Ever since the music had started Maria had been on the dance floor with either her new husband or someone in the wedding party. Lily hadn't really expected to be able to have much conversation with her and was just glad to see her having such a good time at her own wedding.

The next song was slower and when it started, Michael pulled her closer and this time held on to her. Lily looked around the dance floor and noticed that people were all doing a more formal dance.

"Don't worry," said Michael. "Just follow me and you'll be fine. You're a natural dancer."

Lily forced herself to relax and to ignore the pressure of his hand on her bare back and the pleasure that his touch gave her. There was obvious chemistry that was becoming harder to deny. Instead of thinking about all the questions that it raised, she followed his lead and found herself twirling around the dance floor and rocking to the music.

When the song ended the band stopped playing and announced they were taking a break. As Lily and Michael walked across the dance floor, Michael slipped his arm around her and leaned over to speak to her. "You can stop worrying about Irene."

Lily turned to him in surprise. "Why? Has something happened?"

"They've got him in custody."

She stopped walking and stared up at him. "What do you mean? What did you do?"

"When he started harassing Irene he was in violation of probation. He broke the law. All I did was have someone let his probation officer know."

"And then?"

"They went out there and picked him up at his mother's where he's been staying."

Lily shuddered. "I can't say I'm sorry. He really was scaring her."

"And he might have hurt her."

Lily nodded. "Or worse. Thanks," she added, reaching out and giving him a hug. "I don't think I've ever had someone do something so effective before."

He smiled sheepishly. "It's not so difficult if you know the right people."

"Maybe that's true, but most of us don't," she said, grinning at him.

The main course was paella served family style, accompanied by rice and salad. When the band came back from their break they once again played soft

Spanish music as they dined. The tempo picked up when the guests were finished eating, and everyone headed for the dance floor. This time Lily was even more comfortable and quickly lost herself in the music. When Michael reached over and pulled her toward him, she responded without stopping to analyze what was happening between them. When a slow song started and she remained in his arms, she didn't at first think much about it. It was only when she realized the chemistry that had been obvious all evening was heating up and creating a powerful brew that she started to wonder if she should pull away. But Lily did nothing to resist Michael when he pulled her closer and leaned his head against hers, even when she realized that if she turned her head slightly, their lips would meet. She wanted that to happen, God help her, she wanted him to kiss her. She didn't think she could stand it if he didn't. The song came to an end and when the music stopped, Lily let out a soft sigh.

Michael reached up and gently turned her head so that she was facing him, leaned his forehead into hers and stared into her eyes. "I think we have some stuff to talk about," he said softly.

She nodded. "Yeah, I guess we do. But not now, okay?"

Michael gave her a slow smile. "It can wait," he said, skimming his finger across her lips, "but let's not wait for too long."

Chapter Seventeen

The wedding ended about eleven, shortly after the cutting of the cake and throwing of the bouquet, caught by Maria's cousin, the flower girl. As Michael and Lily walked to the car, Lily realized she was exhausted, too exhausted to talk about whatever it was that seemed to be going on between her and Michael.

"About tonight," she said, "can we just not talk about it, at least not now?"

Michael looked over and shrugged. "If that's what you want," he said. He had one arm casually draped over her shoulder.

She nodded. "It's what I want." She had mentally taken note of his arm around her, but didn't say anything about it. Probably, she had to admit, because she liked having him be so proprietary.

"But we can't avoid talking about it indefinitely," he said. "I'm not going to let that happen."

181

"Fair enough," she said. "In fact I totally agree we need to talk, just not tonight. Okay?"

He pulled her into a squeeze and then released her. "Okay."

After that they didn't say much as Michael maneuvered his way through the streets of Paterson back onto the highway for the trip back to Jersey City. He'd switched the radio station to a local mellow jazz station and they rode in almost comfortable silence. Lily must have fallen asleep because the next thing she knew they were in front of her building and Michael was saying her name.

"Lily, wake up. You're home."

Michael walked her to the door, kissed her on the cheek, and gallantly waited while she let herself in. The message light on her phone was blinking. With a mixture of dread and resignation, she punched the buttons and sat down, taking off her shoes as she prepared to listen.

There were three messages. The first was from her mother, who said that she and her father would be going to her brother's in San Francisco for Thanksgiving. Of course she was welcome to go too. Lily didn't want to. Going to California for a weekend would be too expensive, particularly since she didn't think it would be fun. Her mother would want to know what was happening with her and Josh, and Lily didn't want to talk about that yet; certainly not with her entire family.

So she'd have to figure out something else for Thanksgiving. She really didn't mind, Lily realized after a beat. In fact she'd been dreading Thanksgiving, particularly since her mother would be asking about Josh and the status of their relationship. The signs weren't good and Lily dreaded telling her mother that the relationship was over if her suspicions proved to be accurate. She knew her mother had visions of Lily as a doctor's wife and wouldn't be happy to have those visions go up in smoke. Lily was sure her mother had already mentally planned the wedding and wouldn't be surprised if she'd made some calls about places to have it. No, she wouldn't be happy if it wasn't meant to be.

The second message was from Josh. He'd made reservations at a small hotel in Chicago and plane reservations too for both of them to fly there the following weekend. "I put everything on my Amex," he said, "so figure the trip is an early Christmas present."

The last call was from Irene. Lily figured she was calling about Romano. She realized that she was relieved for the distraction so she wouldn't have to think about Josh and the visit to Chicago. Irene called to say she'd heard from the police. "They told me Romano would be locked up for the weekend," she said, "so I can start breathing again. I thought you'd want to know." There was a pause. "I don't know how they knew all about it," she added, "including the fact that it was me that was getting the threats, but it was such a relief to hear that he was locked up."

Lily smiled thinking that Irene had Michael to thank for her peace of mind.

Lily didn't see or hear from Michael on Sunday, which, she tried to convince herself, was just as well.

But she kept thinking back to Saturday—what fun it was dancing and how good it felt to be in Michael's arms. As she watered her plants, cleaned the apartment and took the dog for a five-mile run, she went over every minute of the wedding, savoring each bit. The look on Michael's face when he first saw her all dressed up, how handsome he looked in his dark suit, what fun it was getting to know Maria's cousins and their spouses and how easy it was being with Michael. If Josh had been there instead of Michael, he'd have been quiet except when the conversation was about him, bored because he didn't know anyone and didn't dance. He would have been urging her to leave as soon as they got there. Lily tried to remember what it was about Josh that had made her fall in love with him.

And the dancing! She smiled to herself, remembering. It wouldn't be right to compare how she felt in Michael's arms to what it was like to be with Josh. That would be disloyal. But she couldn't help thinking how good it felt when Michael held her close.

Lily went straight to court on Monday morning to file a petition for custody of the Muniz children. Their mother had been notified and she would be meeting them at the courthouse. As she walked over to the courthouse with Vicky, Vicky explained that Ms. Muniz had finally returned home late Friday afternoon, explaining that she'd asked a friend to watch the kids, but that the girlfriend must have stepped out. Ms. Muniz couldn't remember the name of the friend and was vague about where she lived, but said she would get back to Vicky with that information. As for the children's fathers, there were four of them, according to Ms. Muniz: one was incarcerated, but she wasn't sure where; one was deceased; one had moved back to Puerto Rico; and the fourth had disappeared shortly after the baby was conceived. Lily reminded Vicky to get as much identifying information as she could from Ms. Muniz so they could search for the three surviving fathers. Even if the men couldn't take their daughters, they might have relatives who could. Lily had learned that it was the norm, rather than the exception, in these poor families for fathers to be missing, but that sometimes there were relatives who would be happy to step up to the plate to help out, if needed. From the sounds of it, it appeared that family help would be needed here. Besides, it would be a lot easier for these kids to stay together if they were with family than to find a foster family to take all four girls. Four children were, in Lily's experience, difficult to place together in a foster home, but a grandmother might be willing, particularly if the state helped her out financially.

Lily was thinking about Michael when she walked into the courtroom. He was standing off to the side looking almost as good in his uniform as he had in his navy suit. Her thoughts were interrupted by Tracy.

"Some wedding, huh? And you two. Whew! There was some steam coming from your corner!"

Lily looked up with embarrassment, wondering who else was present in the courtroom. The judge, not yet in robes, had walked in from his chamber. "What's that you're talking about?" he asked.

"Maria's wedding," said Tracy. "Great time, good food, fabulous music, and these two were the big hit," she said, motioning in the directions of Lily and Michael.

The judge looked up and over at Lily not even trying to hide his amusement. "These two?"

Lily shrugged. She might as well bite the bullet and come clean. "I think what Tracy is referring to is the fact that she saw Michael and me together at Maria's wedding."

"Ah," said the judge, continuing to look amused.

Lily tried again. "It just happens that we're neighbors and it was easier than going alone."

"Of course," said the judge, whose mouth was twitching as if to keep from laughing.

Tracy shook her head and muttered—in an audible voice, "Neighbors, huh, an interesting way to describe it."

The judge went back to his chambers to get into his robe. Michael, who, Lily realized, had ducked out during the interrogation, brought Ms. Muniz in and directed her to the far end of the table where Lily was sitting. Vicky had also come into the courtroom. Just as she was about to sit down between Lily and Ms. Muniz the judge's entrance was announced with Michael's pronouncement that they all rise.

When they were told they could sit down, the judge announced the matter for the record, including the docket number, Ms. Muniz's full name, the names of her children's fathers, and each of her children's names. Then it was Lily's turn. She put her appearance on the record before explaining why her office had brought the matter before the judge. As briefly as possible Lily reported that Ms. Muniz had left her children alone, noting the girls' ages. She then asked that Vicky be sworn in as a witness so she could testify about the incident and what she had seen.

After establishing that Vicky had been working as a caseworker for fifteen years and knew the Muniz family as their caseworker for the last three, Lily began to question Vicky about the prior Friday afternoon.

"Ms. Sanchez, did you see the Muniz children Friday morning?"

When Vicky nodded, Lily reminded her to answer the question instead of shaking her head since they were being recorded.

"Yes," said Vicky. "I was on my way to see another client, driving down Broadway, so I was going by their building. I was at a stoplight on their corner when I happened to look up and see the three older girls playing on the roof."

Lily nodded encouragingly. She found testimony worked best when the caseworker felt comfortable and believed she was doing a good job.

"So what did you do?"

"I pulled over, of course. Then I called my supervisor on my cell as I ran to the building." She looked up at the judge explaining. "I needed to call my supervisor so she could call the other client and let them know I might be late or not get there at all." She paused and waved her hands in front of her face. "It didn't take as long as it sounds."

Lily nodded.

"I parked and talked on the phone at the same time. I hurried because I was afraid for those girls, afraid one of them was going to fall off the roof."

"You don't know that," said Ms. Muniz.

"Quiet, ma'am," said Michael as he walked over and stood beside her. "You're not to interrupt."

The judge looked down at her from his bench. "You'll have your chance to speak. But I would suggest that you wait until you have an attorney. You know, you are entitled to a lawyer and if you cannot afford one, one will be appointed for you." He looked down at her over the rim of his glasses, "Do you understand?"

She nodded.

"Do you wish to have a lawyer?"

She nodded again.

"Can you afford your own or do you wish to request to have one appointed?" The judge nodded in Tracy's direction. "She'll assist you in filling out the forms after we're finished with this hearing. In the meantime, I would suggest you listen to what's being said. You'll have an opportunity to respond today, but you might be better off if you wait until you have a lawyer and let him or her speak for you."

"Will that take long—getting a lawyer?"

"No. If I find that the DYFS was correct in removing your children, they will remain in the DYFS's custody and we'll come back to court as soon as possible to discuss what to do next. In the meantime you will be given a court-appointed lawyer." He looked over at

Tracy. "When is the soonest we could come back to court on this case?"

"The week after next," she said, "that's the next available time."

"November 17," said Judge Keegan, "ten days from now."

"And I won't get my children back until then?"

The judge put up his hand as if to silence her. "We haven't finished the hearing yet and I haven't decided whether your children will be put into the state's custody." He nodded in Lily's direction. "Please continue, Counselor."

Lily nodded. "Ms. Sanchez," she said, looking at Vicky, "please tell the court what you found when you reached the roof of the building."

"As I said, the three Muniz girls were up there playing."

"How old are they?"

Vicky paused before answering. "Maria, who is the oldest, is ten. Tiffany is next. She's eight. Angel is six and there's also baby, but she wasn't there." She looked up at the judge. "We arranged day care for her so Ms. Muniz could look for a job. The baby is fifteen months. The others are supposed to be in school."

"And they weren't last Friday?" This question came from the judge.

Vicky shook her head. "I later learned that it was a parent-teacher conference so the girls had the afternoon off. When I questioned them they told me that they'd gone to school and were let out early. Maria said they walked home, found the apartment locked, and went up to the roof to play until their mother got home."

"Did they know where their mother was?" This question was from Lily.

Vicky shook her head. "They did not."

"So what did you do after you got the girls off the roof?" asked Lily.

"I waited with them downstairs on the front steps since their apartment was locked."

"For how long?"

"About an hour." She paused as if thinking. "No," she corrected herself. "It was an hour and fifteen minutes—until two thirty, and then when she still hadn't come, I took the girls back to our office." Vicky looked up at the judge. "But I left the mother a note saying where I'd taken them with my phone number asking her to call me as soon as she got in."

"And did she?" the judge asked.

Vicky nodded. "Yes."

"What time was that?"

"Six o'clock."

"Did she say where she'd been?" Lily asked.

Vicky nodded. "With a sick friend."

"Did she say if she'd known that the girls were getting out early?"

"She said she forgot."

"What time would the girls usually have gotten home?" the judge asked.

"Three o'clock."

"So even if they hadn't been let out early they still

would have come home to a locked apartment," said Lily.

Vicky nodded. "That's right."

Ms. Muniz raised her hand. "I can explain."

"As I said before," said the judge, "you'd be wise to wait until you have a lawyer to speak for you."

She shrugged. "My boyfriend was sick. He needed me. What was I supposed to do?"

Michael walked over and stood next to her. "Quiet, ma'am. Don't interrupt the judge."

There was a moment of silence and then the judge looked over at Lily. "Anything else, Counselor?"

Lily shook her head. "Based upon the fact that these three young girls were left unsupervised and locked out of their apartment and thus exposed to imminent danger, it is our contention that they require the intervention of the state and protective services and we ask for legal custody of them until the court is satisfied that their mother is capable of keeping them safe and can appropriately care for them."

The judge banged down his gavel. "Based upon the allegations of the state supported by the sworn testimony of the caseworker, we find that these children require the intervention of the state and transfer custody to the state until such time as it is determined that their mother has shown that she is able to appropriately care for them."

The judge immediately left the bench. While Ms. Muniz howled, Tracy went over to her and handed her the form to fill out for a court-appointed lawyer. Vicky and Lily stood up to leave the courtroom. Vicky now had the authority and responsibility to find homes for these kids. Lily left the courtroom because she never stuck around for times like this. The last thing she wanted to do was to have a confrontation with a distraught mother. It wouldn't solve anything and could easily cause problems if parents thought they could talk to her.

She was standing outside in the hall buttoning her wool coat when Michael came out and approached her. He grinned sheepishly. "I hope Tracy's remarks didn't embarrass you."

She smiled and shook her head, feeling her face flush in betrayal. "I should have known she would be watching us. It was a prime opportunity for a gossip like her."

He grinned. "Yeah, but still—I don't want you to feel . . ."

She waved her hand and shook her head again.

Michael moved a step closer. "But I do think we need to talk. Will you be home tonight?"

Lily thought quickly. She had no plans, but was she ready for this conversation?

"We can't ignore what happened," said Michael.

"You're right," she conceded. "Come by after seven. I won't be home until then." She had to work late to get ready for court reviews the following day.

When the doorbell rang at seven thirty Lily was almost relieved; now this conversation was going to happen, she was anxious to have it over with. She'd gotten home at seven, walked Sam, changed into jeans, put together a peanut butter sandwich, which she forced down since she was too nervous to have an appetite, and quickly tidied up the living room. In the remaining five minutes, she'd nervously paced. Although there was an obvious attraction between her and Michael, they'd never talked about it and she wasn't quite sure what he'd have to say—or what she would say, for that matter. That she had this longtime boyfriend? But did she? All she knew for sure about Josh was that they were meeting Saturday at the Drake Hotel in Chicago to talk. What did she feel? Attraction for Michael certainly. For Josh? She wasn't sure anymore. He'd been a constant in her life for so long, she couldn't imagine him not there. On the other hand, she'd be kidding herself if she tried to pretend the relationship was in good shape. Not when she'd begun to dread his calls.

Michael had changed out of his uniform into jeans and a flannel shirt. Dressed like that, jeans, work boots, shirtsleeves rolled up, he looked more like a contractor/urban developer than a sheriff and, Lily thought, feeling her breath catch in her throat, very sexy.

When she'd opened the door and stood facing him, their eyes met and she thought her heart would stop. She quickly turned away, she hoped in time, before he saw how vulnerable she was. If he realized she had practically no defenses to him, she'd be lost and that must not happen. There was her relationship with Josh to consider—at the very least, it needed to be resolved. There was also the fact that they worked together and she didn't think her office would look kindly on her having a relationship with the sheriff in her courtroom.

"Is this a good time to stop by?" he asked.

She nodded. "Come on in." She motioned toward the living room. "Want something to drink?"

"I wouldn't mind a beer if you've got one."

"Absolutely," she said as she headed to the kitchen. She thought there was still at least one bottle left over from when he'd been there with his brothers helping her move in her furniture. She knew for sure that there was an open bottle of Pinot Grigio and she was going to get herself a glass of that. Michael's presence and her attraction to him had put her on edge and she was going to self-medicate.

Michael followed her into the kitchen as she was pouring herself some wine. She'd already opened the bottle of beer and taken out a glass to pour it into.

"Don't waste a glass on me," he said. "I'm just as happy to drink my beer out of a bottle."

She turned and grinned at him. "Okay," she said, handing him his beer, the last one, "but I wouldn't have minded."

They took their drinks and the bowl of nuts that Lily set out and carried them to the living room where they sat side by side on the couch, since that was the only place to sit in the room. She leaned as far back as she could to keep some distance from him and tried to relax.

"So," he said, "I guess Tracy saw us together at the wedding."

She grimaced. "I guess we should have been more discreet—or just not have gone together."

He waved his hand in dismissal. "That's nuts. Tracy

is a gossip and a busybody, but that shouldn't keep us from living our lives."

She looked at him without saying anything.

He looked back and smiled. "Besides, she's assuming, if I know our Tracy, that we're already deep into a torrid affair when, in fact, we're only just testing the waters."

She grinned in spite of her anxiety. So that's what they were doing, "testing the waters." She supposed she could live with that. "Maybe so, but what about Judge Keegan? What is he going to think?"

Michael shook his head before taking a gulp of his beer. "The judge knows Tracy. He's not going to pay her any mind."

She looked at him skeptically. "I only wish that were true! You saw his reaction! He was very interested."

Michael had the grace to grin. "Sure he was interested, but not judgmental. He just likes to keep up on what's going on in his courtroom."

Lily made a disgusted noise. "Maybe I don't want them to know what's going on." She leaned back, took a sip of her wine and looked over at Michael who, she suspected, was trying to keep from laughing.

Instead, he grinned and reached over and squeezed her knee, which happened to be the part of her body closest to him and within reaching distance. "Don't worry about the judge. Trust me. I've worked with the man for five years. Although he likes to know what's going on, he doesn't trade on gossip. If there was anything between us, he might know about it, but he wouldn't pass it on. And if it didn't affect how the courtroom operated, he wouldn't care."

"How do you know? Has this kind of thing happened to you before?" Lily kicked herself when the words were halfway out of her mouth.

Michael grinned and cocked an eyebrow. "Jealous?"

Lily shook her head, trying not to look offended. "You certainly don't have to give me an explanation," she said stiffly.

"I guess not," said Michael continuing to smile as he took another pull on his beer. "But I'll tell you anyway." He looked over at her. "I assume you'll keep it to yourself."

"Of course," said Lily after swallowing another sip of wine. She wondered if she was going to want to hear this story. What if it was about Michael and a girlfriend? She really wouldn't want to know.

"Maria and Todd, the probation officer, had something going for a while. No one said anything, but it was obvious to anyone with two eyes. Todd was always hanging around, coming up with all kinds of excuses to visit the courtroom. And then it ended and we never saw Todd again on the ninth floor. After about a month, the judge turned to me one morning when no one was around. He says, 'Guess Todd's not going to come around anymore, huh?' That was all."

"What did you say?" asked Lily, drawn into the story and curious to check out Todd.

Michael shrugged. "Not much. Something like, 'Doesn't look like it.'" He grinned sheepishly. "You know how guys are. We don't dissect these things."

She grinned in response. "Guess that's true. That exchange would never have occurred between two women."

Michael nodded vigorously. "That's my point exactly. The judge is not a woman and Tracy doesn't have any female pals up there to gossip with and we're not interesting enough for anyone outside our courtroom to care." He looked over at her and smiled. "So relax."

Lily let out a long sigh and drank some wine. "I'll try."

"So tell me," said Michael as he put his beer down on the coffee table and took a handful of nuts, "do you know what's going on with us?"

Lily shook her head and tried to ignore the loud thumping in her chest.

Michael reached over and ran a finger down the side of her cheek to her chin, which he cupped in his hand, and then turned her head so that she faced him. "Seems like we should figure that out, don't you think?" He took a swallow of his beer before continuing. "I obviously like you," he said, "and obviously I'm interested in having more to our relationship," he said, "but what do you want?"

She looked into his eyes and felt her mouth go dry. She wasn't sure if she could speak, but she had to. She had to say something.

"There's someone," she managed.

Michael nodded. "I figured there had to be. But where is he?"

Lily briefly explained about Josh and their living apart all these years since college.

Michael shook his head. "I don't get it," he said. "How can he leave you alone like this? I couldn't if I were Josh."

She shrugged. "He always said it was good for our relationship, that it would make the relationship stronger."

Michael looked skeptical. "Do you believe that?"

Lily shook her head. "I used to." But she didn't anymore. If Josh cared and truly loved her, he would have wanted her around. Wouldn't he? She could see that now, maybe because of Michael's reaction and her response to him. A man who truly loved a woman didn't leave her alone. They could have worked something out so they could have been together. Other couples did. But maybe it had been convenient for both of them to have it this way. That was something she would have to think about.

Michael stood up. "I'm going to be a good guy, even if it kills me. I've told you how I feel. When you're ready, let me know what you want to do about it." He paused. "I can be patient while you figure it out. Just don't take too long."

She stood up too, mostly relieved that he was going to make this easy for her, but at the same time disappointed. She couldn't pretend, at least to herself, that she didn't want him. Maybe he read her mind, for he pulled her toward him and kissed her hard before letting her go. As good as the kiss felt, it was really a tease, only making her want more. He headed to the door, turning before he walked across the threshold. "Let me know if it doesn't work out with him."

"I will," she promised, tempted to pull him back into the room, but knowing that his leaving was the right thing—at least for now. She had to figure out her relationships with Josh and with Michael, and as quickly as possible, before things got even more complicated.

Chapter Eighteen

The next morning when Lily was out walking Sam on the block on the other side of Hamilton Park she saw Michael. He was coming down the steps of a building with a woman. Lily and Sam were about a block away and she was just about to call out when she noticed the woman. Even then she was going to run up and say hello, until she realized that Michael had his arm around her. Her steps faltered. When they reached the bottom step, Michael leaned down, pulled the woman toward him and kissed her. Lily froze in midstep and watched the scene, paralyzed. The woman withdrew from the kiss, reached up, and caressed his cheek before turning and quickly walking away.

For a few minutes Lily continued to stare as Michael watched the woman go, then he turned and hurried in the opposite direction to his truck that was parked on the street. At this point, Lily turned and fled back home, desperate not to be seen by him.

She thought back to Tracy's comment earlier that fall about Michael's reputation—a different girl every week. She tried not to feel stupid. What had she been thinking, taking his attentions seriously? He wasn't her type anyway. He was a hale and hearty blue-collar sort of guy. Her mother was right. Josh, the doctor, was more her speed. He might, at first glance, seem a trifle dull and maybe Tracy would refer to him as a dork, but he was a Steady Eddie who loved her.

But for the rest of the day, Lily couldn't get the image of Michael on the steps with that girl out of her mind. She was mad at herself for thinking there might be something between them and preparing to end it with Josh. She'd obviously misinterpreted his interest and their time together, or else he'd left her place last night and had already moved on.

Later that same day when Lily spotted Michael at the courthouse she went out of her way to avoid having to speak to him. She waited until the last minute before actually going into the courtroom so there wouldn't be any chance that they would be alone together. She was there that day because she was filing some motions for guardianship for some teenagers. It was a way to give legal custody to the caretaker without terminating parents' rights. That way if the parents eventually got themselves together they could go to court and get their kids back. Sometimes it was a more practical solution than having relatives adopt their sister's or daughter's children.

After taking care of business, Lily headed straight back out to the street to her car and almost made it when she heard her name being called.

Michael came jogging over. "Heard you were in the building. You have time for a cup of coffee?" he said. "I could probably get a break."

Lily looked straight at Michael, determined not to succumb to his charm. How could he be so two-faced? "I've got to get back to my office," she said. "Got lots to do."

Michael nodded. "What about this weekend?" he began.

Lily shook her head. "I'm not going to be around. I'm going out of town."

"Oh, okay," he said. "What about Sam? Who's going to walk him?"

"Your brothers said they would take care of him. Pat promised to look in."

"You talked to them?" Michael suddenly seemed unsure of himself. "You called to tell them you were going out of town?"

She nodded, desperate to get away from him. He was confusing her with his reaction. The way he was behaving, you'd almost think he was hurt that she hadn't told him she was leaving for the weekend. But from the way he behaved with that woman, that couldn't possibly be the case. She pasted on a phony smile and looked up at him, all the while wishing she wasn't attracted to him. "See you next week," she said. "Have a fun weekend."

"You too," he said, continuing to look confused.

* * *

The flight to Chicago was typical. There was a fast-food snack that the airline called dinner, minor turbulence, and they arrived at O'Hare half an hour late. Josh was waiting for her when she stepped into the terminal. He was standing there, big smile on his face, a bouquet of daisies in his arms. Lily felt confused. Why was he being so nice? In all their years together, he'd never been in the least bit romantic. Why now? Had he done something that made him feel guilty? In any case, the flowers, instead of making her feel loved and cherished, made her feel uneasy and uncomfortable.

Josh grinned and handed her the flowers. "Welcome to the Midwest."

Lily returned his smile as she took them. "They're beautiful."

"And I've got more surprises in store for you," he said as he reached for her carry-on and guided her through the crowds to the exit and bus stop.

He wasn't kidding. When they got to the Drake Hotel, Lily continued to wonder about the obvious extravagance. As long as she'd known him, Josh had been on a tight budget and had watched every penny. This was a first-class hotel. Where had he gotten the money? Why now?

Josh opened the door to the room and pressed her inside. "Voilà," he said, turning and smiling at her. "What do you think?"

She shook her head in wonder. More flowers. At least two dozen white roses and a bottle of champagne chilling in a silver bucket, with two flutes standing by.

"Champagne?" she said. "Did you just win the lottery?"

He smiled, looking very pleased with himself. "Nothing's too good for my girl," he said. "I've been thinking lately that it's about time I let you know that."

"Oh," she said softly and smiled shyly. Hadn't she wanted this?

Josh closed the door to their room after dramatically hanging the Do Not Disturb sign outside. Lily watched him nervously and wished she were more excited. He'd gone to so much trouble and she was feeling guilty over her inability to be more excited about seeing him. Jet lag, she told herself. Things would be just great once she adjusted to the time change.

"Champagne?" asked Josh as he slowly pried off the top of the bottle.

"Of course," she said, holding up one of the flutes for him to fill. She drank it down quickly, hoping it would relax her and make her feel more amorous. She was sure Josh had more on his mind than drinking champagne.

"Let's get comfortable," he said as he put down his wineglass. "Come on," he said, pulling her down onto the bed. "Let's relax and get to know each other again. We've put off our future for too long. It's time to act on it."

Lily took another big swallow of her champagne. Isn't this what she always wanted—Josh's undivided attention? Why wasn't she more excited? "A refill?" she asked, raising her glass. More champagne would relax her.

Josh smiled knowingly as he filled her glass to the brim. "You drink up while I work at making you more comfortable," he said. "My baby needs some tender loving care to get in the mood," he crooned. "Now don't you?"

Lily willed herself into submission and forced herself to be in the moment and to feel his tender fondling. She started to succumb when Michael's face swam into her consciousness. She squeezed her eyes shut and willed him away. Josh was her future, not Michael.

She never completely succeeded in banishing Michael or getting completely into the here and now with Josh that evening, but Josh didn't seem to notice. After he went to sleep, she lay beside him, wide-awake and confused, unable to sleep even though it was one A.M. Eastern Standard Time. A future with Josh is what she'd always wanted. And even if she wanted a future with Michael, it wasn't in the offing.

The rest of the weekend was more of the same. Josh had, for the very first time in their relationship, gone to a great deal of trouble to entertain her. He took her to the Chicago Art Museum instead of the science museum, which she knew he would have preferred. They had dinner at Charley Trotters, a trendy four-star restaurant, after drinks at the bar at the Drake. He was thoughtful, considerate, and hardly talked about himself. The only exception was Saturday night.

"I want to talk about us," he began.

Her heart lurched. She had been dreading this conversation.

"I know the distance between us has been a strain, but

it's almost over; the end is finally in sight and you will see that any sacrifices we made have been worth it."

She nodded, waiting for him to continue. They had not been worth it, as far as she was concerned, but maybe he would have something to say that would change her mind.

"I've been thinking about next year after the fellowship is over," he continued, looking at her across the candlelit table. The waiter had taken their order and poured them each a glass of wine. "I've got two offers that appeal to me. I wanted you to be the one to pick out which of the two it'll be."

"They're definite offers?" she asked, stalling for time.

He beamed. "Yup. I've got two contracts waiting to be signed. And they're both great. One is in San Francisco and the other is here in Chicago."

She must have looked shocked for he held up his hand. "I know," he said. "You want to be on the East Coast near your family. But Baltimore doesn't give me as many options in my specialty and—"

She shook her head and interrupted him. "But Josh, what about my job?"

He smiled as he reached over and patted her hand. "Honey, that's the best part of all of this. You won't have to work."

"What? I don't understand."

"With either deal I'm going to be paid so much money that you won't have to work."

"Oh, I see," she said slowly. "But what if I want to?"

He shrugged. "In that case I guess you'd have to take

another bar exam. But"—and he waved his hand as if brushing away an inconvenience—"you'll be so busy planning our wedding and getting us settled that you're not going to have time to think about that for a while."

Lily squeezed her eyes shut and counted to ten. Wasn't this what she'd always wanted?

Chapter Nineteen

Lily flew back to New Jersey the next morning on an early flight so she'd be back in time for work. Even so, Josh's flight was hours before hers since his rounds began at six. He left her there still half-asleep with a kiss and a promise that they'd see each other at Christmas.

She was unsettled about how the weekend had gone. She tried to distract herself with a romance novel on the flight back. It was about a couple who couldn't live without each other—soul mates who were complete once they met. They managed to stay together in spite of insurmountable difficulties. By the time she landed in Newark, she knew what she had to do and made the arrangements before she left the airport.

As soon as she got to the office she learned that she had to be in court later that afternoon, one thirty, right after the judge came back from lunch. There'd been a removal over the weekend involving a mother who, while intoxicated, had gone to the police station and said she didn't want her kids anymore. They were too much to handle. The police called Lily's office and they took the kids.

She was dreading court. She did not want to run into Michael. She had enough problems sorting out her feelings for Josh, and seeing Michael would just make her feel worse. But she had to do her job. So promptly at one thirty, after reviewing the complaint, she arrived at Judge Keegan's courtroom. Michael was already inside, talking to Tracy. When he saw her, he hesitated before greeting her—as if unsure of his welcome.

"Afternoon," said Lily briskly. "This shouldn't take very long."

"Any parents?" asked Tracy.

"A mother," said Lily. "She's been given notice that we're doing this today so we expect her. There's no father—at least no one who's involved with the kids. We'll get that info from her when she comes in so we can get him, or them—she has three kids—in here the next time we're in court, that is if we can find the guys."

"These people are amazing," said Tracy. "Don't these fathers know they have kids?"

"It's hard to figure out what they know," said Lily. "Sometimes I think the mothers don't always tell them."

Michael came back inside. "There's a Ms. Bryant out in the hall. Is she a party?"

Lily nodded. "She's the mother. Was anyone with her?"

He shook his head. "I'll give her the forms to fill out so she can have an attorney for the next time."

"Thanks. I appreciate it."

When Tracy left the courtroom, Michael came over to her. "What's going on, Lily?" he said softly so as not to be overheard. "Did I do something to offend you?"

"Of course not," said Lily as she shook her head and turned away quickly before she melted under his gaze. One look from him and she'd be tempted to tell him everything. She was not going to humiliate herself. But to make sure she didn't break down and do something stupid, she went to the back of the courtroom where the caseworker was waiting and talked to her.

The case had a better outcome than Lily expected. After Lily put the details of the removal on the record, Ms. Bryant apologized and said it would not happen again. She explained that she had been under an enormous strain because of a romantic entanglement but recognized that she shouldn't be taking it out on her kids. She promised to stop drinking and take better care of her kids. The judge proposed that if she agreed to counseling and went to AA meetings he would give her another chance. She left the courtroom chastened but with custody of her kids.

That night Lily was on a plane to Cincinnati. From there she'd connect with a flight to South Dakota. She'd maxed out her MasterCard buying this roundtrip ticket, but she had to talk to Josh in person.

Five hours later, some of which was spent hanging around airports, she was in the reservation's only taxi, on her way to the hospital, wondering for the first time since she'd begun her journey if she was going to have trouble finding Josh.

Fortunately, she did not. When she got to the front desk at the emergency room and asked for him the woman there checked her charts and confirmed he was on duty.

"I'll have him paged."

Suddenly Lily panicked. Was she being impulsive? Had she thought this through? What she was about to do would affect the rest of her life. Was she prepared for that?

She didn't feel any better when Josh walked through the door. "Lily!" he said when he saw her. "What a surprise! Is something wrong? Are you okay?"

He looked boyishly handsome in his hospital garb, his stethoscope around his neck, just like on television. Numbly she noticed that he wore jeans under his gown and some kind of suede slip-on shoes that she didn't recognize. The fact that she'd never seen him like this—at work, in his element, made her feel sad, but also convinced her that she was doing the right thing.

"Is there someplace we can talk?" she managed to say.

"Sure," he said. "We'll go to the lounge. Just give me a minute to get coverage." He paused, hesitating. "Am I going to need it for very long?"

She shook her head. "No. We'll be done in less than a half hour." He'd never change.

Once they sat down with their burned coffee, which Lily assumed was a hospital requirement, her mind went blank. Mechanically, she opened her mouth and started to speak, willing herself to find the words. She'd come all this way, so she had to do it.

"It's not working," she said. "We're a couple out of habit, not out of love."

Josh just looked at her blankly and didn't respond.

"We don't even know each other anymore," she continued. "Couldn't you see that last weekend?"

He shook his head. "I don't understand, unless there's someone else."

"There isn't." *Not really*, she added to herself, *but at least he made me think.*

Josh moved over closer to her and took one of hands. "Lily, we've been together a long time. Tell me what's bothering you so we can work this out."

Lily sighed. "You're not listening to me, Josh." She looked up at him, conscious of her hand in his and desperate to remove it, but afraid to make this worse than it had to be. "I realized after last weekend that although you and I are going through the motions of being in a relationship, we're not anymore." She removed her hand. She had to do this right. "It's been over for a while now." She leaned back to give herself some distance and be able to look directly at him without feeling slammed by his nearness.

"But we had plans," he said.

She nodded. "We did—plans that we made in college. But that was—what—five years ago? A lot has happened since then. You've changed. I've changed. We've both grown—but our relationship hasn't."

He looked hurt—or puzzled—she wasn't sure which, but she thought it was finally sinking in. "Josh, think about it! We haven't put anything into this relationship in years. We've gone along just assuming it was fine when in fact it probably doesn't work for either of us except to eliminate the need to meet anyone else."

He looked at her suspiciously. "There's someone else, isn't there?"

She sighed. "Why did you decide to invite me to Chicago?"

"What do you mean?"

"I'm talking about the sudden invitation. We weren't scheduled to get together until Christmas. We never see each other spontaneously."

Suddenly he exploded. "There's someone else, isn't there!"

She shook her head. "That's got nothing to do with it."

"I should have known," he screamed.

She interrupted him. "I came all the way out here to talk to you face-to-face. If you can't do that without making a scene, I'll call you later and we can do this over the phone."

He looked like he was about to explode again, but then he seemed to get ahold of himself. "Okay. I don't want you to go. You did come all this way . . ." His voice trailed off. "But"—he looked around—"this isn't the place. Let me see if I can get out of here for a bit. Wait outside in the lobby while I check."

She sat in the lobby for what seemed to be forever, but was really only five minutes, dreading his return at the same time that she wanted to get it over with. What part of breaking up didn't he understand? But Josh was never much of a listener. Why would he start now?

When he appeared, he was obviously even more agitated than he'd been in the lounge. "I've been thinking about what you said," he snarled. "The only explanation is a new guy in your life. Otherwise, you would have gone along with my plans. You always have."

They were walking on the grounds of the clinic. Lily stopped and stared at him. "Part of what you say is true. I have always gone along with your plans. And maybe there is someone in my life that I could be interested in, but that doesn't change the fact that this latest plan of yours doesn't take into account that I have built a career in New Jersey. If you cared about me, loved me— which, by the way, you haven't said for so long I don't remember the last time you did—you would have taken my life into account when you were planning, instead of just thinking about yourself.

"But more importantly, it's obvious we don't love each other. If you were honest, you would see, like I have, that whatever was between us has been over for a long time."

He didn't say anything for a bit. When he did speak, it was through gritted teeth. "I shouldn't have to keep saying I love you. It should be obvious. And for whose benefit do you think I have been working? You'll be sorry, Lily Hanson. Whoever this new guy is, he won't be me and before long, you'll realize your mistake. But don't kid yourself into thinking I'll wait, because I won't. There are plenty who would love to get their hands on me. Believe me."

Chapter Twenty

When Lily got home to her apartment in Jersey City it was nearly ten at night. She was exhausted. It had taken almost the entire day to get back. She hadn't spent all that time in the air. There'd been a layover in Houston and to save money she'd taken the train from the airport to Penn Station in Newark and the PATH from there to downtown Jersey City, which took another hour.

Sam was excited to see her and she scratched his head with one hand as she leafed through her mail that Patrick had left on the counter in the kitchen when he'd stopped by to walk the dog. There were only bills and department store circulars that she quickly discarded. She didn't have any money to spend. As she placed the bills back on the counter to pay later, she noticed that the message light was flashing. She looked at it with dread. Had Josh called to scream at her some more? She didn't want to hear it and was tempted to ignore the flashing light and go straight to bed. But what if it was someone else? What if it was important? She'd better check. The first message was from Josh. He sounded drunk and was even more abusive than he'd been in person. She erased the message before she heard the end of it. The second message was from Irene. She sounded scared. Stuttering and breathless, she asked Lily to call her.

Sam would have to wait for his walk until she found out what Irene wanted. "What's happening?" asked Lily when Irene answered on the first ring.

"It's Mr. Romano. He's calling me and threatened my children this time," said Irene. She sounded desperate.

"Romano, the one who beat up his wife? Wasn't he in jail?"

"Yes. But now he's out. He can't find his wife so he's calling me. Says it's my fault that he was in jail and blames me for breaking up his family. He says he's going to come and get me and get my kids." Her voice broke as she said the last words.

"Are you alone?"

"No. My kids are here."

"Your kids." That made it even worse. "Your kids, huh," she said, trying not to let Irene know the panic she felt.

"Yes, that's right."

"Anyone else there now?"

"No," said Irene, "just me and the kids."

Lily struggled out of her coat as she tried to think. There had to be neighbors, family. "Is there someplace you can go tonight?"

Irene sighed again. "My parents are in the Dominican Republic. So is the children's father. We're not together, though he would help if he was here, but he's not." She said something inaudible to one of her children and then was back on the phone. "I've only lived in Passaic for a few months. Before that I lived in Clifton. I don't know anyone around here."

"Well, let's try not to panic," said Lily for her own sake as much as for Irene. "What exactly did he say to you?"

"He said it was my fault that he had nowhere to live, that he lost his kids." Her voice broke. "He said he was going to make me sorry." There was silence for a moment. "He said he was going to get my kids, Lily!" she cried. "How am I going to protect them? This man is a monster!"

"It's going to be okay," said Lily trying to sound confident and certain. "You're not alone in this."

Irene was quiet for a moment. "But I am."

"No," said Lily. "I'm here. We'll figure out what to do together."

"Please. I don't want anything to happen to my children."

"I know." Lily considered their options. "You call the police?"

"Yes."

"What did they say?"

"What you said, file an order of protection. But that's not going to stop him."

"No, of course not, and even if it were, we need to do

something to protect you tonight." She was quiet for a moment. "Let me make some phone calls and see what I come up with."

"Okay," said Irene. "But you'll call me back?"

"Of course, as soon as I can." She'd have to. Irene was frightened and with good reason. Lily wouldn't let her fend for herself.

She got off the phone and continued to pace around the living room, trying to think. She reviewed the situation from every angle and kept coming up with the same solution. She had to call Michael.

When he answered on the fifth ring he sounded half-asleep. Lily realized how late it was and that she'd probably awakened him. She apologized.

Even half-asleep it was clear that he was surprised to hear from her. "Something wrong?" he asked.

"Yes, but it's not me," she said quickly. "It's my caseworker, Irene. Remember that guy who threatened her? The one we got in jail when he violated the restraining order? Jose Romano?"

"Sure. I remember him well. A dangerous dude if there ever was one." Michael was waking up.

"That's the one." She was relieved he remembered. It made this call less difficult since he knew that Irene was in real danger. "Anyway, he called her at home. He's threatening her again."

"And she's alone."

"Exactly."

"Anywhere she can go?"

"No."

"No family, no friends nearby?"

"Unfortunately not," said Lily.

"Would you take her in?"

"That's what I was thinking, but he doesn't like me any more than he likes her."

"Right, but he doesn't know where you live, does he?"

"No. I'm sure he has no idea."

Michael was silent for a minute. "How about I go get her and the kids. They can bunk in with you tonight and tomorrow we can get Romano back in jail where he belongs. It shouldn't be too difficult since he's on parole and by harassing her, he is violating that order of protection she filed."

"Sounds like a plan. I'll call her now. Make sure she's willing."

"Call me right back," he said.

Lily quickly dialed Irene's number. When she answered, Lily quickly filled her in with the details of the plan.

"You'd do that for me?" asked Irene.

"Of course, I'm not going to leave you out there. So you agree?"

"Sure. When will he be here?"

"I guess as long as it takes him to drive over there. I'm going to call him back now and let him know you agree with the plan. Meantime, get yourself and the kids ready."

Lily finally took Sam for a walk after she called Michael and told him it was a go. By now Sam was desperate and had gone so far as to bring Lily the leash as if to make sure she understood what he wanted. Back in the apartment she unpacked her overnight bag, changed the sheets on her bed since she planned on putting Irene and her kids in her room, and checked her fridge for breakfast food. Fortunately she had the makings for pancakes and enough juice and coffee.

Michael didn't come in when he dropped them. Instead, he called her from the car and told her to open her front door since they were on their way in. Lily didn't blame Michael for avoiding her. After all, she'd been avoiding him all week. Even so, she felt a pang of regret that it was so. But she put all such thoughts out of her mind and focused on the more pressing responsibility of her guests.

Sam probably saved the day, or at least distracted Irene's children from the crisis they were in the middle of. Even Irene looked more relaxed when Sam started to race around the living room barking with excitement while Irene's two kids egged him on. The downside was that it was an hour and a half before the kids settled down and they and Irene were finally to bed. After Lily got them tucked away in her room and made up the pullout couch, she was ready to crash. Bed was looking awfully good after the long day. Besides, she hadn't slept very well the night before after talking with Josh. Not that she thought she had made a mistake, but breaking up with the man she'd dated for so long was still traumatic.

Lily heard a light tapping at the front door while she was in the middle of washing her face. She rinsed off the face wash, patted her face dry, threw a bathrobe over her nightgown and went to see who it was. She didn't think it could be Romano. He didn't know where she lived and was too much of a coward to come by if he did. But to be safe she looked through the peephole before she unlocked and opened the door.

It was Michael. In spite of herself, she felt a tingle of excitement when she saw his face through the opening in her door.

"I wanted to make sure you were all right," he said when she let him in.

She pointed to her closed bedroom door, behind which Irene and the children were sleeping, and put a finger to her lips to remind him to keep his voice down.

"I gave them my room," she explained. "I thought they would feel better if they were all together."

Michael nodded. "Good idea. They were pretty shook-up when I brought them over."

Lily nodded. "But Sam calmed them down," she said.

Michael looked around the room. "Where is he now?"

Lily grinned and motioned toward her bedroom. "With his new friends. When we put them to bed he piled in along with them as if he was part of the clan." She paused. "I won't hold it against him. They need him right now a lot more than I do and I guess he must miss kids. There were some in his last home." She sighed. "I feel kind of bad."

Michael grinned at her. "You could always get some."

"Kids you mean?" she said, returning his smile. "True. I could adopt—more efficient than having my own and I happen to know of a few who are available.

Sam wouldn't have to wait until they grow up to play with them."

Michael cleared his throat and looked over at the couch. "Can we talk?"

She hesitated. It had already been a big day for talks. Was she ready for one more? Did she really have a choice? "I guess." She walked over to the couch and moved her blanket and pillow to the side to make room to sit down.

Chapter Twenty-one

"You have anything to drink?" asked Michael. He almost sounded nervous.

"Of course. Want a beer, or wine? Coffee?"

"A beer sounds good," he said. "Do you want one?"

She shook her head. "I'll have a glass of wine, I think." Maybe it would help ease the tension that was very much present.

He followed her into the kitchen. She handed him a beer, glad that she had picked up a six-pack for Pat when had looked after Sam while she was gone. She hadn't expected him to really have one, but at least it was there if he wanted. Lily poured herself a glass of wine and offered Michael a glass, which he declined. They brought their drinks out to the living room. He sat down on a chair he had brought in from the kitchen and she sat across from him on the couch.

223

"You wanted to talk," she reminded him when he didn't say anything for a bit.

"Yes," he said, taking a deep swallow. He put his glass down on the table in front of the couch and turned to her. "What's going on?"

She took a small sip of her wine before she spoke. "What makes you think there's something wrong?" she stalled.

He rolled his eyes and sighed. "Lily, don't play games. It's obvious."

She wasn't going to tell him until she could figure a way to do it without sounding stupid or as if she were spying on him. But she didn't have a plan of resistance except to stonewall him. "How so?"

He sighed again.

She wasn't fooling him one bit.

He leaned back on the chair, took another long swig of his beer, put it down and crossed his arms. "I'm not going to leave until I find out what's going on, so if you want to make it hard just be aware that it will take a lot longer." He looked at his watch. "I don't know about you, but I've got all night. I slept in this morning and I'm not due at work tomorrow until noon, so if it takes all night, that's okay by me."

She glowered. Could he know that she'd been up since five? He couldn't, so she'd tough it out because there was no way in hell she was going to tell him that she was mad at him because she thought something was developing between them until she saw him with another woman. It was just too humiliating.

Neither said anything for a bit and though she was sorely tempted to break the silence, she did not.

"I can see I'm not getting anywhere," he said finally, "so I'll start." He cleared his throat. "Since Maria's wedding, and maybe even before that, something's been building up between us." As he spoke, he did not look at her. Instead he leaned forward and with his hands clasped together and stared straight ahead. Then he looked over at her. "Correct?"

She nodded, but did not say anything.

"You told me that there is a guy in your life and I let you know that I respected that and would back off, but I also said I'd be around if you changed your mind." He looked up at her to see her reaction. "Correct?"

She nodded again.

"So why for the last week and a half have you been avoiding me?"

When she didn't answer, he continued. "I can see that you're going to make this harder than it has to be." He looked at her, but she still said nothing. "I'll give you the benefit of the doubt and figure that you have your reasons."

Her reasons were starting to feel silly. He was here, wasn't he, reminding her that he cared. Shouldn't she tell him about seeing him with that woman? Maybe she should give him a chance to explain. But now that they were here sitting across from each other, she felt so silly and so vulnerable. If she was wrong about that woman, she would look awfully insecure. And what if she were right?

"When you come down to it, even though you've met my family and we see each other at work, there are a lot of things we don't know about each other, right?"

She nodded and took another sip of her wine. It was true there were a lot of things they didn't know about each other—like who was that woman she saw him kissing?

He continued, more at ease, she noticed, sitting back and looking over at her straight in the eye. The beer must be working.

"When it comes right down to it," he repeated, "I hardly know anything about you. You never really talk about yourself. Fact is, most of what I know about you is what I've observed in court." He reached over and touched her face, turning it so she faced him and looked directly into his eyes. "Do you realize that you have never really talked about your personal life with me?" He waited a beat for her to answer and when she didn't, he continued. "I know there's this longtime boyfriend, but he's never around and doesn't seem to intrude on your life at all. I know you have a couple of brothers, a mother and a father, and that you don't seem close to any of them. I also know you have a former roommate who moved to Boston and is getting married next spring."

Lily started to mention Arlene, but Michael interrupted her. "Yeah, that other one who's so negative with the computer geek boyfriend, but you know what I mean." He leaned forward and put his elbows on his knees. "So what gives? What do you want from me? Friendship? Romance? It's your choice, but I need to know and in a clear concrete way. I'm no good with this subtle stuff."

There was a long awkward silence during which Lily tried to figure out how to answer him. Michael shook his head and gave her a crooked grin. "You're really going to make me do all the talking?"

She nodded, returning his smile. The knot in her stomach that she hadn't realized was there had started to thaw. It was going to be all right. She'd get through this conversation and maybe it would be all right.

Michael took another swig of his beer, noticed it was almost finished and got up for another one, glancing at her glass to see how she was doing on her wine—she had plenty—and came back with another and sat back down. "I'm figuring you're sorting out this long-distance romance or just over it. I also figured until last week that you were interested in getting into something with me." He looked up at her questioningly.

"Maybe," she said with half a smile.

"Then what happened?"

She sighed. Obviously she was going to have to talk. Not to would be childish. But first she had some questions of her own. "What about you? Much of what you've said about me also applies to you. I've met your family, but I've never seen your apartment. I don't know your friends. And you're a good-looking single man. I'm sure you've had your conquests, surer because of your reputation."

This time he really smiled. "My reputation?"

"Yeah," she said, trying not to sound defensive. "People talk."

"People talk," he repeated. He grimaced. "By people, do you mean Tracy?"

"Maybe," she allowed. Shoot. Had Tracy made up the stories about his reputation just to cause trouble?

He must have read her mind. "Would it surprise you to learn that Tracy might have a reason to spread gossip about me?"

She shrugged. "I don't know." Why had she ever believed Tracy?

"Tracy and I went out," he said, "very briefly, a year and a half ago." He looked up at her and shook his head. "I know, don't say it. One of the dumbest things I've ever done. I can only imagine what you're thinking."

"I didn't say anything." And she didn't know what to think. Tracy was attractive, but she was also a bit of an airhead and mean-spirited to boot—but Lily had believed her about Michael, hadn't she?

"Yeah, but your face is very expressive," Michael said. "Something you should know about yourself, Counselor."

Lily filed that tidbit away. Expressive faces weren't good when you were a litigator, particularly when you were bluffing.

Michael continued, "I have good reason to believe that Tracy has mythologized my reputation as a cad about town." He looked over at her. "Correct?"

Lily grinned. He did have her there. "So when did you get so good at cross-examination?"

"I've observed the best," he said, returning her smile.

Lily shrugged and took a sip of wine. "Tracy didn't tell me she'd been in a relationship with you. She just warned me about your womanizing ways." She smiled when she said the words, hoping he wouldn't think she'd taken Tracy seriously, though it was obvious that she'd given Tracy some credence.

"Okay, so Tracy warned you about me. No big surprise. Which explains why it may have taken you a while to warm up to me, but then you got to know me. We went to the wedding together. We hit it off. It was after that that you gave me the brush off. Want to explain?"

She sighed and took a gulp of her wine, and then another, while she thought about what to tell him. She hoped to find the right words so she didn't look suspicious or insecure, but she did want to know the identity of the woman she saw with him.

"You're right about my questioning my long-term relationship," she said. "I have been."

"Well?" he said, waiting expectantly.

She sighed again. "I guess I should explain." She tried to figure out where to begin as she settled back on the couch, tucking her feet underneath and leaning back on her pillow to be more comfortable.

"Josh," she began and then looked up at Michael. "His name is Josh Morgan. He's just finishing up a postdoctoral program doing research at an Indian reservation out in South Dakota. Before that he was a resident in San Francisco after he was in medical school in Chicago. We met in college in Boston our junior year."

Michael looked puzzled. "But you guys haven't been together—I mean lived in the same city—for how long?"

She grimaced. "Since college. And therein lies the problem, or at least some of it. We've lived apart all those years and neither of us minded or took it as something strange. And maybe, to be fair, it wasn't in the beginning." She shrugged. "The upshot of it is that now we don't even know each other." She took a sip of her wine while she tried to collect her thoughts and figure out what Michael should and needed to know about her and Josh and what was just stuff that was best forgotten or at least kept to herself.

She continued, "We met junior year and fell in love. Saw each other over that summer because we were both working at the beach in Maryland. He's from D.C. and, as you know, I'm from Baltimore. We continued to be a couple our senior year and talked about long-term stuff, but we also had our own ambitions. I wanted to go to law school and he wanted to be a doctor." She looked up at Michael. "At that point, I guess, it seemed early in the relationship to decide what school we'd apply to based upon where the other was going. We both wanted to go to the best place that we could, which is why he landed in Chicago and I ended up in New York."

She paused and took another small sip of wine. "I really can't explain the rest of it. I've been thinking over the last few days how it came to be that I've stayed in a relationship with someone who I never see for all these years and I don't have a good explanation except to say that it must in some way have worked for me too." She looked up at Michael and shrugged. "It gave me my freedom to do what I wanted. For one thing, I got to focus on my career."

He shook his head. "But it surprises me that you never met anyone during those years."

She shook her head. "In law school we were still very close and my relationship with him probably saved me from getting into something stupid while I was there, but you're right about the time after that. In hindsight, it makes no sense. Being committed to him just kept me from getting involved with other people."

"So what's changed now?"

She grinned sheepishly. "Well, I'm sure my getting to know you had something to do with it. Even though things really haven't progressed very much, it looked like they might and I'm not good at duplicity."

He returned her grin. "That's nice to know."

"Maybe it goes hand in hand with having an expressive face. I would have been found out."

He got up from the chair and settled himself on the couch next to her. He reached over and squeezed her hand. "Works for me," he said. He let her hand go and then put his arm along the back of the couch in such a way that his hand rested on her shoulder.

She looked up at him and smiled. It worked for her to have him so close. This wasn't an easy story to tell and it was nice to feel his comforting touch as she told it.

"So he went to Chicago and you came to New York and then what?"

She leaned back on the pillow and stared at the ceiling. "This is where, I think, it gets crazy. When Josh finished medical school and was deciding where to go for his residency, I fully expected him to apply to something around here. It could have been New York, New

Jersey, Connecticut, or even Philly—all good choices. He did apply to some places nearby, but when it came time to choose, he picked California. We discussed it and even argued about it, and he even suggested that I go out there." She looked over at Michael. "But that didn't really make any sense and even at the time, I knew he was just saying that to placate me. For me to go to California would have meant taking another bar exam or finding a non-lawyer job and leaving everything that I had worked for. He wasn't suggesting marriage then, though that was the underlying plan, but not then." She shook her head. "So we continued as we'd been and when this thing came up in South Dakota it was just more of the same. I didn't even argue with him."

"Weren't you starting to feel as if maybe this relationship wasn't working?"

"Probably when I thought about it, but it had also become a habit. And my mother loved him, or to be more accurate, loved that he was from a fine WASP family and going to be a doctor."

He grinned. "Does that mean she wouldn't be crazy at the idea of her daughter dating a first generation Italian who's a sheriff?"

"Maybe," she said. She found it interesting that he would say they were dating. Was that what was happening? What about the woman she saw him with? She still needed to find out about that.

But it was a distraction having him this close and in spite of her misgivings and reservations, she didn't object when he scooped up her feet, put them on his lap, and started to massage them. She could get used to his ways and assuming there was no other woman in his life, what her mother thought or might think, she realized, did not have the same power it once did.

"Anyway, as you can probably guess since you and your brothers are so much a part of my life these days, I've hardly seen Josh at all these past few months. He came out once and I went out to Chicago to meet him last week." She paused and looked over at Michael, comparing the two men, and realized Michael's gentle strength made Josh's self-absorption so unpalatable and must have played a part in her decision whether she'd been aware of it or not.

"While I was out there, Josh told me that he'd decided that it was time for us to be together and to marry," she said, explaining about their meeting. "I didn't object, because I didn't know what to say. I felt like it had come out of the blue since as far as I was concerned we were steadily growing apart. But when I did think about it on the flight home, I realized I didn't want that anymore. That it was over between me and Josh—probably had been for a while, but I just hadn't noticed it," she added ruefully. "I flew to South Dakota yesterday and told him."

Michael shook his head. "I can understand the law school–med school business. You were only four hours apart then. You could visit each other on weekends."

She nodded. "That had been the idea, though even back then it didn't quite work that way. Josh always seemed to have a reason why we shouldn't see each other that often." It had in fact been her expectation, but when it came down to reality, they saw each other about twice a semester. She started to get mad about that all over again and then reminded herself that it was over.

"What I don't understand," Michael said, "is why he would risk losing you now when you could have been together." He looked at her questioningly. "Didn't he realize how lucky he was?"

She shook her head, embarrassed and angry that she'd obviously not been appreciated. She tried to get up off the couch to escape his close scrutiny, but Michael reached for her hand and held her in place beside him. She started to pull away when he turned her face toward him. Then when he pulled her closer she froze. Even so he did not back off. Instead he gathered her up into his arms and kissed her. When he did, Lily felt whatever tension was left inside her evaporate.

"Do you know how long I've wanted to kiss you? Have you in my arms?"

She shook her head, smiling up at him. He looked so sexy—his dark, hooded eyes focused only on her. He ran his fingers down the side of her face, across her mouth.

Suddenly his phone rang. "Damn," he muttered as they abruptly pulled apart at the jarring sound. He reached into his pocket and when he found the phone flipped it open to answer it.

He listened for a moment. "You want to meet me down at the police station right now?" He listened a moment more and then disconnected his phone. He looked over at her. "They've got Romano."

"Thank God," she said. She'd sat up, away from him.

Michael stood up. "Romano went to his house and was holding his wife and kids hostage."

"But they got him. The kids are okay?"

He nodded. "Yeah, everyone is fine, just shook-up. The police surrounded him and forced him out. They didn't have to use their guns."

"Why do they want you?"

"To fill them in on the threats that he made to Irene. She'll have to go down to the police station tomorrow, but for now it'll work if I tell them what I know." He looked over at her. "When we talked earlier they said they wanted you or Irene, and I convinced them that it could wait until tomorrow, but they need something now to explain the arrest."

She nodded gratefully.

They were standing now facing each other. "You should be okay now that they have him," he said.

"You're right about Irene. The good news will keep until the morning," she said. "I might as well let her sleep." She glanced at her watch. It was four o'clock. She couldn't believe her eyes. Had she really been up for almost twenty-four hours? As far as her personal life went, it had certainly been an eventful twenty-four hours.

Michael took her in his arms and gave her a long hard kiss. Just when she started to respond, he pulled back and grinned as he looked down at her. "We have unfinished business," he said.

She raised an eyebrow and nodded.

"You free tonight?" he said, glancing at his watch.

"I think so," she said.

"Let's talk later about getting together."

She nodded twice as she walked him to the door and watched him get into his car and drive away.

Chapter Twenty-two

The next day was Friday, thank God. Lily didn't expect to have to be in court and had hoped to be able to hide in her office and get some paperwork done. The sleep deprivation from the night before was taking its toll. But when she got to work they told her about an emergency removal. "It's a family matter," Aggie, one of the supervisors in the DYFS office, explained when she called. "Two teenage siblings got into a fight. Not unusual. The problem is that they are being cared for by their older sister because their mother is deceased and their father is in jail. What makes it even more complicated is that the older sister is nine months pregnant. She's due any minute. Anyway, fight was typical. Someone throws a dish and before you know it somebody gets hurt. There's a trip to the emergency room, the police are called, and bingo, we're involved."

"So what did we do?" asked Lily. She hoped, for

once, they'd told everyone to calm down and make up so they could all go home.

Aggie sighed. "Jessica, the big sister, says she doesn't want her little sister back."

"Do you think she means that, or did she say it in anger?" asked Lily.

"Oh, I'm sure she'll get over it and change her mind," said Aggie, "but right now she is mad so Monica, the younger sister, had to be placed in foster care." She paused before adding that there was also a younger brother.

"So what about him?" Lily asked. "Did you have to place him in foster care too?"

"Ronnie? He wants to go with his uncle. Says he's tired of these females always fighting."

Lily smiled to herself. It was so true. Some of these kids really had it tough. "So at the very least," she said, "we have to file on Monica. I assume you're telling me this morning because it needs to be done this afternoon."

Aggie laughed. "Got it on one. It really happened early Thursday morning so I figured we've got to be in court before the weekend. I heard about Irene. I'm sure you're tired, but I didn't have a choice but to call you."

"That's fine," said Lily. "It's my job. Besides, this sounds pretty straightforward. But the judge will want to hear it by three o'clock since it's the beginning of the weekend."

"No problem. Someone will e-mail it to you shortly."

When Lily got to the courthouse she didn't see any sign of Michael. She felt as if she had on her "Michaelsensitizer" and would know if he was anywhere in the vicinity. She wasn't sure if she was ready to see him— not with other eyes upon them, particularly Tracy's. Naturally Tracy was the first person that she encountered when she went into the courtroom.

"Judge has the complaint," said Tracy. "Are any parents showing up?"

"No parents, we've got the caretaker, an older sister, who they tell me is coming, but I didn't see anyone out in the hallway."

Tracy sighed audibly. "You know the judge likes to leave early, so they better get here soon."

Lily nodded. There was nothing more irritating than underlings who were more demanding than their bosses. Fortunately the caseworker walked in at that moment.

"Are the parties here yet?" asked Lily.

Alex, who was the caseworker, nodded. "The sister and her boyfriend just got here."

"Good." Lily looked up at Tracy. "We can begin anytime."

Tracy sighed again. "Now we just have to wait for Michael and the judge is on the phone," she said, pointing to the lit button.

Lily felt her face heat up when Michael walked in. She quickly looked over at Tracy to see if she noticed. Fortunately, Tracy's attention was on the computer screen in front of her. It wouldn't do to give Tracy any more reason to suspect there was something going on between her and Michael. She was glad that Michael hadn't given anything away when he walked in, just giving her a brief nod.

The sister came in, looking very pregnant, her belly bulging out between her tight T-shirt and her jeans. Lily mentally crossed her fingers that the stress of being in court wouldn't throw her into labor. She was glad the woman's boyfriend, who she assumed was the father, was with her.

Michael looked over at Lily. "Want him here?"

She shook her head. These proceedings were confidential and the man, though apparently supportive of his girlfriend, the caretaker, had no legal relationship to the minors involved. Michael explained all this to the boyfriend and asked him to wait outside in the hallway. He agreed.

The judge walked in. Lily, the caseworker, and the sister stood until the judge motioned for them to sit and the proceedings began with Lily questioning the caseworker about the circumstances. Once the grounds for filing were established Lily made it clear that the agency did not want to punish the sister for trying to care for her siblings.

"Your Honor, we see this as a case of a young woman having too much on her plate. As you can see, she's nine months pregnant and had the responsibility of raising her brother and sister. We are not here to criticize her or to punish her for trying, but to help. Our plan is to place her sister and brother with others while she cares for the new baby. If and when she feels she wants to have them back with her she will have that opportunity. But right now we just want her to focus on the upcoming event and wish her well."

The young woman flashed Lily a grateful smile.

Judge Keegan looked down at her from the bench. "That okay with you?"

She nodded.

"Seems to me," said Judge Keegan, "that the best thing we can do for this woman is dismiss her from this action so she doesn't have any record to explain later. How about I grant your office legal custody of the kids so you can take care of them and leave her out of it completely?"

Lily nodded. "That works for us." She was reminded, not for the first time, of how lucky she was to appear before a practical and sensible judge who also had a big heart.

When the proceeding ended and the defendant and caseworker had left the courtroom and the judge was off the bench, Michael walked over to Lily.

"We still on for tonight?" he said, his voice barely audible.

Lily quickly glanced over at Tracy and nodded without speaking. Tracy was shutting down her computer and didn't seem to notice. Even so, Lily didn't say anything, but instead packed up her own papers and waited for Tracy to leave.

When Tracy's computer was off she glanced over at Lily and then Michael, who was lining up the chairs in front of the counsel table. "Well I guess I'll head out," she said. "Michael, don't forget to turn off the lights."

"No problem."

Tracy hesitated, again looking from Lily to Michael, then shrugged and walked out of the room, shutting the door behind her.

Deborah Nolan

Michael looked over at Lily and smiled. "How are you doing today?"

"A little tired," she said, returning his smile.

"So how about coming to my place for dinner? I was thinking about what you said—that you have never even seen my apartment—and we never finished our conversation. I still don't know why you've been avoiding me. How about I make you dinner and we can talk."

Lily hesitated. What would she be getting into? She didn't trust herself to resist him but could she trust him? She still needed to find out. She looked up at him as he stood there looking down at her, waiting for an answer and knowing she wouldn't be able to resist him. He was beautiful and when he smiled and looked at her with those dark blue eyes she melted. But what was to be gained by not going? Her heart would stay intact, and her virtue too. But she might never find out who that girl was that she saw him with and she might never have the chance to taste his kisses or be held in his arms.

She looked up at Michael. "What time?"

"Is six too early? Mom wants us to come by for a drink. She asked us for dinner but I said we had plans— so we'll just drop by and then go to my place. I can pick up what I need for dinner on my way to pick you up."

She grinned and shook her head. "How'd you know I was going to say yes?"

He had the grace to look sheepish. "I was hoping. As for my mother, she likes you a lot and is always asking if you and Sam are coming. She assumes we're dating and I haven't dissuaded her of that fact."

Lily smiled to herself when she heard that.

Lily was able to go home directly from court, so she was there by five, which gave her time to shower, change, and walk Sam. She didn't have to get dressed up for her date with Michael but she wanted to look her best. After scanning her closet, she decided on a short denim skirt, leggings, and boots. With the skirt she wore a skinny knit top she'd picked up on sale when she was shopping in the City. This would be her first chance to wear it. She looked good and very hip, she decided as she surveyed her image in front of the mirror. She was glad. She had a good feeling about tonight and wanted to look special.

Shortly after that the doorbell rang. Lily opened it to find Michael standing there. He looked irresistible and she suspected he hadn't even tried. He had on worn jeans that nicely hugged his body and the blue chambray shirt that she loved. He wore the shirt with sleeves rolled up and the top two buttons open, revealing a few light brown curly chest hairs.

"All set?" he said.

She nodded, grabbed her purse and keys, and they were off.

"Hope you like pasta," said Michael as he helped her into his Jeep. "It seemed the best plan under the circumstances. I got some nice red wine and some cheese to snack on while we wait for it to cook."

"Sounds perfect," she said.

On the trip over to his mother's they continued to talk food. He obviously knew his way around the kitchen and pasta sauces. To her relief, the looming question of why she'd been avoiding him was not addressed. She was beginning to feel pretty silly about it even though it would have to be addressed. Although it was a necessary conversation, she wasn't sure where it would lead and if there would be anything left when it was over. She liked being with Michael and didn't want that to end. She was afraid that when they finally did talk about that woman, anything that had started between them would fall apart.

Michael's mother greeted her warmly. "I'm sorry you and Michael can't stay for dinner," she said. "I've got plenty, if you change your minds."

"Mom," intervened Michael, "I told you we've got plans."

His mother sighed. "I won't say another word. But at least sit down and have a glass of wine that your Uncle Vito made. It's quite good and I got some of that asiago cheese you always like."

The three settled in with their glasses of wine that really wasn't half bad. Michael told his mother about the night before and Lily sat back enjoying—even if it turned out to be pretend—being part of a warm family who cared about one another.

Patrick and Anthony were on their way over along with a cousin Theresa whose husband had just shipped out to Iraq.

"She's so upset," said Ms. Frascato. "I wish there was something we could do." She turned to Lily. "She just found out she's pregnant with twins and he's on his way to the other side of the world risking his life. We're all praying he gets home safely and in time to see them born.

"That must be them now," she said at the sound of a door opening, followed by voices, Pat's, Anthony's, and a woman's.

"We're back here," she called out. "Put away your coats and come join us. Lily's here."

When Theresa walked in, Lily had to make an effort not to show her relief. She was the woman she'd seen Michael with the week before. The one she had been sure he was having an affair with. But as relieved as she was, she also felt silly and knew she would have to come clean with Michael. What should she tell him? That she immediately jumped to the conclusion that he was involved with someone because she saw him walking with her? In spite of her relief, Lily inwardly winced.

She waited until they were back at his place to bring up the woman. After he gave her a quick tour of his apartment, which was a cozy but basic bachelor pad, she told him that they needed to talk. Lily wanted to get the conversation over with before she did something stupid—like fall in love with Michael. Even if she wanted to forget about it, Michael hadn't. He'd brought it up on the ride over to his place so she would have to fess up. Then if he had issues about the way she'd jumped to conclusions, she'd deal with it.

"Now let me get this straight," said Michael. "You thought I had something going with Theresa?"

"Yes," said Lily. She couldn't bring herself to look at him when she told him what she'd thought and instead had started chopping up the olives Michael had measured out, which were to go into the sauce. She continued chopping, head down. "I saw you with her, your arm around her, coming out of a building near Hamilton." She looked up at him for a moment and then back down at the olives she was working on. "When I saw you kiss her and give her a big hug before the two of you parted, I assumed."

Michael's arms suddenly came around her from behind. He took the knife out of her hand and after placing it down on the counter, turned her around to face him. He cupped her chin with his hand and raised her head so she was looking at him. His eyes were crinkling and looked like he might laugh. Instead he pulled her close to him, squeezed her hard, and then led her to the couch.

"Let me see if I understand this," he said. He was sitting close to her and had turned so they were facing each other. "You thought I had some sort of romantic thing with Theresa and that bothered you."

She nodded without saying anything.

"You were jealous?"

"Michael, stop. This is embarrassing enough. You're making it worse."

"Sweetheart, I'm sorry," he said, pulling her close

again. This time he didn't let go. Instead he pulled her legs up over his so she was practically in his lap. He continued to hold her close. "I guess I'm flattered," he said. "Does that mean you care for me?"

"Maybe," said Lily.

"So it's okay if I let you know that I've been falling in love with you?"

She looked up, afraid to believe what she heard. "Really?"

He looked down at her with his eyes that were warm and intense, all amusement gone. He nodded. "Really. Almost since the moment I met you. Certainly from the time you moved over here. I haven't known what to do about it, except to see you as often as I could and try to figure out what you thought about me."

Lily looked up at him, amazed at his honesty. He loved her. He loved her! And she hadn't even known.

"I thought I was getting through to you—that maybe something was starting to develop when we went to the wedding together. But then you started to give me the cold shoulder and we were back to square one." He smiled and hugged her again. "So when you tell me that maybe you were jealous, I have to admit that it makes me very happy."

"You know I had no idea about any of this," said Lily.

"I know. I thought about saying something on the way back from the wedding, but you didn't want to talk about it and then you fell asleep. I could have woken you, but I guess I lost my nerve."

By now Michael was kissing her. First her fingers, one by one, then her chin, her eyes, and then her mouth.

Deborah Nolan

She felt herself sink into the kisses, enjoying the feel of his touch and her body's response to him.

"Could you love me?" he asked as he paused between kisses.

"I already do," she said.